GUIDEPOSTS

GUIDEPOSTS

CHURCH CHOIR
MYSTERIES™

The
Unsuitable
Suitor

Nicola Furlong

Guideposts®

CARMEL, NEW YORK 10512

www.guidepostsbooks.com

www.guidepostsbooks.com
Series Editor: Michele Slung
Cover art by Stephen Gardner & Edgar Jerins
Cover design by Wendy Bass
Interior design by José R. Fonfrias
Interior cat illustrations by Viqui Maggio
Typeset by Composition Technologies, Inc.
Printed in the United States of America

*Dedicated with love and admiration
to my dear "other" parents:
Pearl and Richard Turner*

Acknowledgments

I WOULD LIKE TO THANK my brother-in-law, Edward Praught, and Colin Savage, of C&S Motorcycles in Sidney, British Columbia, for their Norton Commando motorbike information. Also, special thanks to Elizabeth Kramer Gold, the managing editor at Guideposts Book & Inspirational Media Division, and Michele Slung, the series editor extraordinaire of "Church Choir Mysteries." And, as always, to Glynne Turner.

The Unsuitable Suitor

A REN'T *YOU* TWO the lucky ones," Gracie Parks said, eyeing the two teenagers who were hunched over her kitchen table, devouring homemade gazpacho garden soup. She'd been experimenting with a variety of chilled meals and had found this recipe particularly tasty. "Lucky to be spending the last part of your summer vacation with your favorite aunt!"

The girls, Brooke and Emma Reynolds, barely nodded. Their spoons caught the stream of August sunlight that poured through the window. Gracie's uncle, George Morgan, grunted, then added a few more croutons to soak up the last puddles in his bowl. "Never thought I'd like cold soup, but this hits the spot, especially in this heat," declared the man affectionately known to one and all as Uncle Miltie.

Marge Lawrence's face beamed with pleasure. She was thrilled to have her fourteen-year-old nieces staying with her. Thinking about what the long, busy days ahead held in store was simply too exciting. "We're going to have all kinds of fun, aren't we, girls?" The twins—fraternal, but equally appealing—flashed smiles. "Shopping, renting movies . . . making new friends. There's lots to do. I . . . I might even try roller-blading."

Gracie glanced at her best friend in alarm, but Marge was too elated to notice. Gracie shivered involuntarily. Last week, while washing breakfast dishes and enjoying the sidewalk antics of her cat Gooseberry, she'd gotten the fright of her life. John Griswold, another neighbor, had suddenly zoomed by, mouth open, arms flailing. Her running shoes had barely hit the front porch when John screamed, swerved to avoid the alarmed pumpkin-colored feline, and crashed headfirst into Mrs. Finkmeyer's cedar hedge. Fortunately, the only damage was a blow to his pride and a dent in Hallie's shrubbery. And he was half Marge's age!

Watching her friend sip her coffee, Gracie began to relax. Really, the whole roller-blading notion was ridiculous! She tried to imagine Marge, with her perfectly coifed hair, painted nails and designer outfits, wearing a helmet, wrist and knee pads. Maybe if they came color-coordinated and with a little tasteful embroidery. She suppressed a chuckle.

"We're going to work in Aunt Marge's gift shop," Emma was saying, her soup bowl finally empty. "It's going to be sooo cool. Like, she's got the neatest stuff!"

"Yeah," her sister added. "From all over the world."

Marge smiled warmly. "Nieces are the best. Aren't they, Uncle Miltie?"

Blue eyes twinkling, Gracie's uncle laid down his spoon with a flourish, replying, "If these two fine young women give you half the love and support that my Gracie gives me, Marge, well . . . then I'd say you were one of Willow Bend's— no, make that one of Indiana's—richest residents."

"Oh, Uncle Miltie, you just say that because I keep you well-supplied with half-gallons of your favorite ice cream flavors!" Gracie laughed fondly. A former building contractor, Gracie's uncle had moved in with her not long after his wife of fifty-six years, Doris, had died. Her own dear Elmo had been called to God five years earlier, so Gracie was open to the companionship, as well as to her uncle's need for her. They had quickly forged a strong and caring relationship. As she rose to give him a hug, she knew she'd have a hard time imagining her life without him. They were the kind of odd couple that really wasn't so odd after all, once you realized what sort of spirit infused them both and how, together, they made so many aspects of their community richer for their presence.

From a safe vantage point above the refrigerator, Gooseberry popped open his eyes. He'd heard a favorite word—ice cream—and wanted to be ready just in case an opportunity arose to lick a carton.

Gracie began to clear the dishes. Brooke jumped up to help out as Gracie returned with a plateful of still-warm chocolate chip cookies.

Marge laughed and poured more milk. "See, girls? Treat your relatives right and you'll be amply rewarded."

Brooke pushed a blonde lock from her eyes and smiled shyly. Gracie couldn't help noticing that her fingernails were bitten to the quick. Her chestnut-haired sister, Emma, grinned, then took a gulp of milk. "Mrs. Parks, why'd you call him Uncle Miltie?"

"It's a nickname, dear," Gracie began, passing the cookie plate. "After a very funny man named Milton Berle, who was famous on television way before your time. You see, my uncle has an inordinate passion for . . . well, Marge, how should I put it?"

"Corny jokes! Just like his namesake, this Miltie knows millions of them. Don't you?" She rolled her eyes at Uncle Miltie.

Their cookies suddenly forgotten, the teenagers stared at the elderly man. "Tell us one, *please*?" they asked in unison.

Like a true showman, he rose slowly, bowing ever so slightly to his audience. "Well, let's see," he said, enjoying his audience's rapt attention. His face brightened. "I've got it! Why did the aunt tell her nieces not to drop the cookies?"

Marge and Gracie exchanged a bemused glance. The twins shook their heads. "We give. Why?" Emma asked impatiently.

14

"Because chocolate chips."

There was silence.

"Get it?" Uncle Miltie looked at them, winking.

"Oh . . . brother!" Marge groaned.

Gracie sighed and shook her head.

Emma blinked. "Hey, yeah. I get it!" She reached for another cookie and bit hard. "Pretty bad, Mr. Morgan."

"Call me Uncle Miltie," he said, snatching his third cookie before sitting down.

Brooke smiled again. "I liked it," she said, picking out a chocolate chip from the soft dough and popping it into her mouth. "Know any more?"

"They're *so* different," Gracie said, handing Marge the large wooden salad bowl. "I know they aren't identical but, somehow, when you hear the word *twins*, you think, *the same.*"

Her friend nodded as she carefully patted the bowl dry. "They've grown so much in the past few years. I hardly recognized them! Oh, Gracie, you of all people understand how difficult it is to be part of their lives when they live on the other side of the country. I really want this time to be special." Gracie did know. Her son Arlen lived in New York City with his wife Wendy and their small son, little Elmo.

Through the kitchen window, they could see the two girls and Uncle Miltie settled happily in the shade on the front porch, engrossed in a game of Scrabble. Nearby on the old-fashioned glider, Gooseberry snoozed. Emma's laugh drifted in through the screen.

"I think it's a little awkward for them, sometimes," Marge continued, gently shutting the window, her voice now a whisper. "Adele has worked very hard to treat them as individuals but . . . they're the same age, in the same class . . . there are bound to be comparisons. It's really a blessing that they don't look alike. Emma's the spitting image of my little sister. Not just her dark looks, but she's just as chatty, outgoing and confident."

Gracie paused as she opened a cabinet to stow some plates. "I'd say the apple doesn't fall far from the tree, or should I say aunt?"

Marge looked affectionately at her friend.

"So, Brooke takes after her father? He was a salesman, wasn't he?" Gracie could see that her childless friend was pleased to think Emma resembled her, but she was curious about the girls' dad.

"Uh huh. Brett. Poor guy. He wasn't very successful. Quiet and shy, just like Brooke. Sales was absolutely the wrong thing but it's what he wound up in, so they just scrimped along." She stood, looking in the direction of the porch. "When Brett lost his job, he was devastated. The girls were only nine and already Adele was working part-time." She sighed. "She quickly became full-time, and I thought that they'd be okay. Her income took the pressure off, or that's how I saw it, but . . ." Marge shook her head.

"Brett didn't see it that way."

"Right. I guess he felt threatened. I don't really know, but slowly he became discouraged, then depressed. Try as he would, he couldn't find a job that suited him . . . or lasted. One day, Adele and the girls came home and he was gone. Left a note saying that they were better off without him." They looked at each other, wordlessly. Marge's expression was the one Gracie recognized as her most worried.

"They haven't heard from him since. But I know they miss him."

"Naturally," Gracie agreed, then asked, "Didn't Adele remarry?"

Marge nodded. "She's about to. And I'm absolutely thrilled for her! Rex is a wonderful man. I think he'll be a caring husband and a fine stepfather. Every child deserves to have two parents in her life. A mother and a father who live in harmony with each other and with their children.

"But?" Gracie asked, letting her friend tell the tale in her own time. Some of it was coming back to her, but mainly, when Marge had talked about her family, she had preferred the happy stories about the twins' successes to the less cheerful ones about their father's failures.

"I . . . I'm not sure how the girls feel. They're reluctant to discuss their father. But they seem to get along with Rex, even if they've refused to take his name." She tapped a bright pink fingernail on the tabletop. "That says something, doesn't it?"

But what? Gracie had to wonder as she followed Marge out to the porch. What are Brooke and Emma trying to say?

CARTER, HONEY, are you sure you're all right? Your voice sounds a little strained." Gracie pressed the telephone receiver closer to her ear, listening carefully. Uncle Miltie was in the living room, glued to the television set's current offering, and it took some concentration to block out the loud, invisible voices.

"I'm fine, Aunt Gracie, really," her niece replied, but she seemed unconvinced. "Probably just a bad connection. Don't worry. I . . . I just thought I'd call and chat for a bit. But enough about me. What's the choir up to? Is Estelle still going for the blue ribbon for impossible divas?"

They both laughed. Though Carter Stephens lived in Chicago, they enjoyed a close relationship, speaking regularly by phone and visiting one another as frequently as possible.

Gracie was so proud of the young assistant district attorney, the first lawyer in her family!

In fact, given that Gracie and Elmo had been blessed with only a son, Gracie loved, cherished and knew Carter as though she were her very own daughter. Which is why she was concerned. This was the third phone call in less than a month in which Carter seemed not her usual self. Of course, there had been past conversations when she had seemed a bit distracted—even a couple of hasty ones where Carter admitted to being run off her feet—and Gracie could well imagine the hectic lifestyle of today's young people, especially that of a lovely, twenty-eight-year-old, big-city assistant DA.

It was a different world from Willow Bend, with highways and high-rises, and neighbors who didn't even know one another.

Should she push for more information? After all, Carter had called her. Gracie sighed. It was so hard to tell over the phone. At times, even with her own son, Arlen, she had difficulties reading his voice. *Well, Lord, do I or don't I? I don't want to be a pest in my niece's life, but if she's troubled or in trouble, I want to help.*

Gracie couldn't decide how to handle it.

"Aunt Gracie, you still there?"

Uncertain and not wanting to press too far, she reluctantly accepted her niece's attempt at changing the subject and finally responded. "All of us Eternal Hopers are fine, though short a few voices for recent practices. Tish and Tyne have been on holiday, and Don's been busy helping a former student, a farmer." She added dryly, "And Estelle's the same as ever."

Carter's soft chuckle quickly warmed Gracie's heart. *Maybe, Lord, it isn't anything serious. Perhaps, she's just a little tired, after all.*

The young woman's voice was suddenly stronger. "A farmer? What in the world does Willow Bend's favorite chemistry teacher know about farming?"

It was Gracie's turn to laugh, as she tried to envision her handsome baritone friend milking cows or collecting eggs. She leaned back in her kitchen chair. Immediately, Gooseberry jumped into her lap and began kneading. She rubbed his orange ear and was rewarded with a rumbling purr. "It seems he knows a bit about fertilizers. His former student, Dennis McIver—you remember Eleanor, who helps me with catering sometimes?"

"Oh, yes. An old woman, *much* older than you. Lives on a farm."

Gracie smiled inwardly at her niece's generous age comparison. Well, maybe not *that* generous, given that the seventy-two year old farmer's wife was a decade her senior. "That's right, dear. Well, Dennis is her grandson. He graduated from agricultural college in the spring, and Eleanor and her husband decided to give him a piece of their acreage. Seems he's trying to grow something called 'designer' lettuces and vegetables. Don thinks it's a good idea, but Dennis's father's and grandfather's reactions are another story altogether."

"You mean produce like arugula, white eggplant and purple broccoli? Well, I'm with Don on this one! That stuff's all the rage in fancy restaurants here."

"Oh? Been to many of them, have you?" Gracie teased. "With anyone special?"

Carter laughed. "I take myself! Look, I've got to go."

"You're still coming for the Blessing Service?" Though they had discussed this already, Gracie wanted to be sure. Carter shared Gracie's love of animals, so the upcoming special Sunday event was an ideal lure. Eternal Hope had been inspired to stage the service by an article in an old *Guideposts* magazine. An Anglican pastor in northern England had started an annual tradition of having his congregation bring their pets—furry, finned or fanged—to be blessed.

"You know, I said it sounded like a terrific idea. But we're spread a bit thin here due to holidays and so I have to wait before I commit."

"You'd just love it," Gracie couldn't help trying to convince her.

"Oh, Aunt Gracie, it's not that I don't *want* to, but work's really—"

"Crazy. I know, honey, but you don't *sound* well. And you know, you're no good to anyone when you're exhausted. It's not this Sunday, but next, remember? It's going to be a lot of fun. We're working on some new songs and I'm catering, and, really, I could use some help! Marge is too busy. Her nieces are visiting. It would be a nice break for you, and I promise not to work you too hard."

"Well... I'm not sure." Carter paused. Gracie silently whispered a prayer. "The Sunday after next, you said?"

She's weakening! "That's right, dear, but you could come earlier?" Gracie decided to go for broke. "So, I'll expect you sometime next week. What about a party? Something low-key but lively." That would be another way of taking Carter's mind off her demanding work schedule, plus whatever else was bothering her.

Carter hesitated again. "Well... I can't commit, but I'll try. Okay? Now really, I've got to go. Love you. Kisses to Uncle Miltie and Gooseberry."

"God bless you," Gracie replied.

But the line was already dead.

T

HERE'S A CHURCH *in the val—ley by the wild wood. No love—li—er spot in the dale.*" Despite having bunions on both feet, there was nothing Gracie liked better than walking and singing the praises of the Lord. Add to the scenario the cool silence that draped the early summer morning— especially lovely after a hot and breezeless night of fitful sleep—and the heady fragrance of nearby tumbling sweet peas, and you get heaven—or as near as Gracie Parks expected to find in this life.

Though Willow Bend was not the town of her youth, it was the community where she and Elmo had made lifelong friends and raised a handsome and bright son. It was where she had lived the longest and felt the most at home.

"No place is so dear to my child—hood, than the lit—tle brown church in the vale."

As Gracie rounded the corner onto Cherry Street, she was

in high gear. Twenty feet in front of her, Gooseberry poked his head from behind a thatch of daisies, then moved along until distracted next by a discarded bit of string. Immediately, his orange body lengthening and tail twitching, the big cat became a hunter. Gracie, meanwhile, pounded on, her voice in rhythm with her stride.

As she finished the old hymn and began her cool-down, her thoughts turned to the upcoming special service. When she had originally read the charming description of how the small English village celebrated the lives of the Lord's precious creatures, she had immediately pictured in its stead her own town and her own pastor, Paul Meyer. And indeed, when she had presented the idea a few weeks ago to the Eternal Hope Community Church, the Board of Directors had just as immediately shown their enthusiasm.

But now, Gracie had begun to have doubts. She paused for a moment to lean on a neighbor's fence and wipe the perspiration from her brow. *Dear Lord, with so many other ways to serve You is this truly what You want us to do? I want to believe it was Your hand, and not mine, that picked that particular magazine and flipped immediately to that specific page. I love all Your creatures, and I know that You do, too. We humans are blessed by each and every one of them, that's for sure, but . . . do they belong in a church when many of Your children are aching for Your spiritual embrace? Our Board has talked and talked and we're still uncertain how exactly to go about this. How could we possibly welcome every loved pet and still keep each one under control? I'm afraid the whole thing could turn out to be a travesty and not the celebration we intend.*

Now moving slowly, she crossed the street in front of her house, stopping to do a few concluding stretches. Gooseberry was on the front porch, huge green eyes staring up at her. Waiting. "Goosie! How'd you get here before me?" she asked, ruffling his neck. "Are you sitting here so prettily, trying to tell me something?"

He opened his mouth in a soundless meow. Very unusual. Gracie bent over, scooped him under her arm and strode inside. "I'll take that as a yes."

A familiar male voice floated outside from the kitchen. The scent of fresh coffee tickled her nose, and Gracie heard her uncle laugh as she pulled on the screen door.

"Don!" she cried out in delight. "Well, this is a lovely morning treat!"

Don Delano jumped up from the kitchen table, almost knocking over his coffee mug, and gave her a quick hug. "Hope you don't mind my dropping by so early? The heat got to me last night and I couldn't sleep. I finally went for a long sunrise walk by the river and eventually found myself climbing your front porch."

"Of course not," she replied. "You know you're always welcome." She glanced at her uncle. "Have you had breakfast?"

Uncle Miltie shook his head. "I was just putting the coffee

on as Don arrived." He placed his mug on the table. "I thought we'd have some cereal."

Gracie was starving after her own exertions, so she could imagine just how ravenous Don was. "Why don't you two start with that while I have a quick shower? Then I'll make us all a real breakfast."

Don, who had just returned to his seat, rose again. "Oh, no, Gracie. I didn't expect breakfast. Honest." His handsome face flushed slightly. "A cup of coffee's more than enough."

"Nonsense! Uncle Miltie and I often have bacon and eggs. It's no trouble to cook a little extra, and we'd love to have your company—"

A loud meow interrupted Gracie, making them all laugh and turn their heads. Gooseberry was crouched in front of his bowl, the tip of his tail jerking impatiently. "Don't worry, sweetie," Gracie said, pouring out his food. "I haven't forgotten about you." She added fresh water to his dish, then patted him on the head.

During the brief time it took for Gracie to shower, change and run a comb through her short red curls, the two men had eaten their cereal and rinsed the bowls. She found them standing side by side at her cutting board, dicing leftover cooked potatoes for hashbrowns.

In a jiffy, she put the bacon on to fry and selected half a dozen eggs. Uncle Miltie began slicing bread while Don finished setting the table and poured fresh cups of coffee.

"Over easy?"

Don nodded.

While she turned the bacon and watched the eggs, Gracie asked, "How's the farm experiment going?"

Uncapping the strawberry jam, Don grinned. "Great guns, I'd say. It took a while to get the right pH for the soil. We experimented a bit, but now the stuff's growing to beat the band."

Uncle Miltie took his plate from Gracie. "Anyone buying it?"

Don accepted a full plate, nodded and cut into a slice of bacon. He chewed for a moment. "Dennis has done a fine job of marketing research and a number of restaurants are interested, but . . ." He paused for a sip of coffee. "This being his first year in business, they're still a little leery of the quality of his produce."

"How in the world does he decide what and how much to grow?" Gracie asked. "I wouldn't know where to start." She dipped her toast into an egg. "Every year, when my new seed catalogues start arriving, I just get more and more confused. There seem to be so many new plants and vegetables, it makes my head spin."

Don cleaned his wire-rimmed glasses. "You've hit the nail on the head, Gracie. Gourmet restaurants are a cut-throat business at the best of times, subject to whims like West Coast food fashion and the latest dietary craze. Makes it very difficult to know in advance what products you're going to need. But if you have the right ones, you can do very well. After a lot of study and thought, Dennis simply decided to try a wide variety, hoping that he'd strike a chord with several."

"Sounds familiar," said Uncle Miltie, pushing his empty plate aside. "That was great, Gracie. Thank you. Anyway, Jake Helms, an old war buddy of mine used to live in Washington State. He's dead now but he was an apple grower, like his father and grandfather before him. For years, he cultivated a few basic types, you know, Macintoshes and Red Delicious, that sort of thing. Then someone introduced the Spartan, I think it was, and a few other new varieties, and everything seemed to change. Folks got a taste of something different and suddenly the old standards no longer suited." Uncle Miltie shook his head, then drained his mug. "He eventually gave in. Said he couldn't keep up so he sold out."

The three sat in an uneasy silence for a few moments, broken only by the occasional soft sounds of Gooseberry's morning ablutions.

Finally, Uncle Miltie cleared his throat. "That's not to say Dennis McIver won't succeed. No, sireee. Jake was old, and he didn't have the energy nor the inclination to tackle change. But Dennis . . . Dennis is young, bright, energetic—why, I've seen him go all out exhibiting at the fair. If anybody can do it, he can!"

"I wish we could convince Dennis's dad and grandfather." Don rose and carried some dishes to the sink. "That was delicious, as always, Gracie. Thank you."

"You're most welcome. So they're unhappy?" Gracie asked.

"I'll say. They think Dennis is plumb crazy. They aren't familiar with the produce he's trying to grow, and they don't understand the markets he's trying to reach . . ." Don paused, then glanced at Uncle Miltie. "I think Ben, in particular, is like your friend, Jake. An old-school kind of guy, who just keeps farming and growing the way he's always done, despite the increased costs and shrinking profits. Farming's changed. Dennis is just trying to adapt. Ben doesn't understand."

Gracie smiled. "Ben's a good farmer, Don, and often more creative than most. After all, he and Eleanor raised six sons on the fruits of their hard labor—and their dairy farm's still a success."

"Uh huh, Gracie. But it's different now, if you're starting out."

"Maybe," Gracie said. "But from what you've said, I think this is an apple that hasn't fallen that far from the tree!"

4

GRACIE LOVED BEING in her garden. Whether she was resting, planting or even weeding, the dazzling colors, tantalizing scents and captivating shapes never ceased to delight and rejuvenate her. She felt safe, surrounded by many happy memories. "The best place to find God is in a garden," her mother used to say, quoting George Bernard Shaw. "You can dig for Him there." And so she did.

Gracie's mother had been blessed with a green thumb and had grown much of her family's produce, but she had always reserved a small, sunny patch where she especially tickled the soil for her cut-flowers: zinnias, sweet peas, love-in-a-mist, wallflowers. Just recalling the old names filled Gracie with a fragrant nostalgia.

Though not quite as gifted as her mother, she managed to combine hard work, natural fertilizers and proper watering to produce gratifying results. Add Uncle Miltie's penchant for pruning and the outcome turned out even more impressive.

The August sun burned ever brighter as she and Uncle Miltie puttered around the front yard, deadheading hollyhocks and geraniums, propping up daisies, and collecting lupin seeds. Gooseberry was snoring lightly under the hydrangeas. Every now and then, his white paws jerked. Gracie had read somewhere this was a sign of dreaming, like rapid eye movement in humans.

This particular morning, Gracie was finding it difficult to concentrate. Her mind kept wandering, bumping into tiny flickers of worry about Carter. And when she pushed those anxieties aside, misgivings about the Blessing Service slipped in. Especially now that Marge's hands were full with the twins, she was going to have to enlist some new help.

And fast.

"Think you've used enough twine?" Uncle Miltie casually asked, tossing seed pods into a jar.

"Huh?" Gracie replied, blinking. She looked down, her hands moving automatically, and burst out laughing. Her poor daisies were trussed up like some terrified hostage! "Oh, dear," she said, unraveling yards of twisted string. She started over, whipping the twine once around the dangling plants and tying it against a stake.

"Penny for your thoughts?" her uncle asked. He slowly

propelled himself up the steps and into the shade. In a moment, he'd settled into the glider.

She sighed, stuffed the remaining ball of twine into her pocket and plunked herself down beside him. "It's nothing, really. I'm just a little worried about Carter. I know she's hiding something—I can hear it in her voice. Call it aunt-ly intuition, but . . ."

The elderly man looked at her quizzically. "Maybe you're just imagining it? She's probably merely over-worked. A job like hers is no walk in the park."

Gracie nodded, trying to conjure up exactly what about her niece's tone had troubled her so.

"Has Carter said anything?" Uncle Miltie prodded her now.

"No," Gracie admitted reluctantly. "It's more what she *doesn't* say that worries me."

"Why don't you give her another call tonight, see if you can convince her once and for all to come for that visit? If nothing else, you'll feel better for having tried."

Gracie wiped the dirt off her pants.

"But that's just the half of it, right? What else?"

She glanced at her uncle, then gave him a quick peck on the cheek. "How'd you know?"

He grinned and pointed to the lawn. Half of the dead-headed geranium cuttings had blossoms!

"Why didn't you stop me?"

He reared back in mock alarm. "Are you kidding? I didn't dare get between a lady and her pruning shears!"

Before she could reply, the phone rang.

Gracie sprinted into the kitchen. "Hello?" she said, partially out of breath.

"Mrs. Parks? This is Rebecca—Becky—Baxter."

"Oh, yes, Becky!" Gracie slipped into a nearby chair. "It's so nice to hear your voice. I was at the bank last week, but your father didn't mention you were home."

"I wasn't. Just arrived a few days ago."

"Have you accepted that job at the bank—oh, dear, I can't remember which one—in Chicago? Your father told everyone at our church's board meeting about how his eldest daughter was following in his footsteps. He's so proud of you!"

There was a long silence. Finally, Rebecca sighed and replied in a flat voice, "It was First Chicago. And no. I haven't accepted it."

"Oh," Gracie said, uncertainly. She remembered Becky as a serious little girl in pigtails who loved Sunday School, especially when Gracie would huddle the children into a storytelling circle. Then Gracie recalled her as a gangly teenager, her braces flashing when finally coaxed to smile. She had lost touch when Becky had gone off to college but had been kept abreast of her progress by her doting parents.

"That's kind of why I'm calling you, Mrs. Parks. I've been going crazy trying to decide about the job. My mom suggested

I get out of the house, get involved in something. You see, all my friends are working and . . ."

Gracie didn't know where this was headed. "I'm not sure what I can do, Becky, but you know I'd be glad to help."

"No, no, you've got it wrong, Mrs. Parks. *I* want to help out. My mom was telling me about the Blessing Service." Her voice grew stronger. "She's planning to bring Brodie and Sammy, and, well, you know how much I love animals. Could I be involved somehow? I'll do anything, make phone calls, hand out flyers, whatever you need. I'd really appreciate it."

"You'd appreciate it?" Gracie laughed. "My dear, you're the answer to my prayer, that's what you are." *Thank You, dear Lord. I'm sure You had a hand in this.* "Are you free in an hour, by any chance? I'm meeting Pat Allen at the church. We've got a lot to do and you could be a tremendous help."

Becky promised said she would be there. As Gracie hung up, her uncle entered the kitchen. Gooseberry strolled behind.

"You look happy," he commented, with a smile.

"Thrilled," she replied, washing her hands. "Becky Baxter's offered to help with the service. Ready for a quick bite? I'm meeting her at the church in an hour."

She turned and started to laugh.

Uncle Miltie was already rummaging eagerly in the fridge while Gooseberry pawed impatiently at his empty dish. Her menfolk were nothing if not singleminded.

WHEN GRACIE STEERED her old Cadillac, Fannie Mae, into the parking lot at Eternal Hope Church, she wasn't surprised to see Pat Allen's vehicle already in its usual parking spot near the walkway. As church secretary, Pat came and went on her own schedule. Her efficiency was unparalleled, and it occasionally worked to offer her snatches of free time. Never one for idle hands, however, she often volunteered elsewhere and particularly enjoyed working with seniors. In fact, Pat's organizational skills, when put into action, had been known to whip into shape most of Willow Bend's golden-age institutions, simultaneously terrifying their staff.

Gracie's beloved place of worship gleamed in the sunlight. Though its building was a century old, Eternal Hope's congregation had taken it over only in the sixties when the

Presbyterians moved. Eternal Hope was originally founded in 1945, the day the Second World War had ended. Gracie always felt the timing to have been wonderfully fitting: from the destruction, chaos and evil of war blossomed renewal, order and goodness. She had been a part of its community ever since her arrival in Willow Bend, and not a day slipped by without her heartfelt prayers of thanks.

"Everything all right, Mrs. Parks?" a voice asked.

Startled from her reverie, Gracie jumped. "Becky! Oh, hello, dear." She hugged the young woman. "I'm sorry, I didn't hear you. Yes, of course, everything's fine. I was just admiring our church."

Rebecca Baxter walked beside her. "You know? They have some impressive churches in Chicago, but I still like ours." She eyed the white vinyl siding. "It looks pretty good, doesn't it? You'd never suspect there was an addition unless someone told you."

Gracie smiled, admiring her young friend's fine features and slim body. "You look wonderful, dear! All grown up." Becky smiled shyly. "And yes, the builders did a good job of joining it all together. When I think of how little room there was originally . . ." She shook her head and climbed the back stairs. "I can't imagine not having the kitchen, extra classrooms and Family Activity Center."

Becky chuckled. "Well, I haven't been to Sunday school in

a while nor used the Activity Center, but I know I speak for the entire congregation when I say we're all thankful for what you do in the kitchen."

They found Pat in her small office, hidden behind a computer screen. "Oh, Gracie, come on in," she said, without looking. "Be with you in a jiffy." After a moment, her narrow face peered around the screen. "Becky? Is that you?" The young woman nodded. Pat smiled, rose and gave Rebecca a warm hug. "Blessings! And welcome home!"

"Blessings to you too, Mrs. Allen."

Gracie said, "Becky's offered to help with the service."

Rebecca nodded enthusiastically. "I said I'll do anything. Filing, running errands, answering the phone. Just put me to work."

Pat shook her head. Rebecca hesitated, uncertain of the secretary's reaction. Even Gracie was taken aback.

"You're a writer, aren't you?" Pat asked.

"Well . . . yes," Becky admitted hesitantly.

"And computer literate?"

Becky grinned. "Born with a mouse at my fingertips."

"My dear, you're a gift from heaven!" Pat shoved a handful of papers at her and gestured toward her chair. "Do you think you could take a stab at drafting a flyer advertising the Blessing Service? I've tried, but . . ." She shook her head again. "I'm much better at numbers."

Within seconds, Becky had settled in behind the computer

screen and was reviewing Pat's suggestions. Her fingers danced over the keyboard as Gracie and Pat sat discussing the service at a nearby table.

"Has Paul decided upon his sermon?"

Pat shook her head. "You know Paul—always striving for that deeper meaning. He needs to do more than just keep people's attention or even tell a good story."

Gracie nodded. From the moment he'd arrived in Willow Bend, Pastor Paul Meyer's sincerity, eagerness and devotion had quickly won the hearts of his congregation. "I know. He takes his vocation so seriously. We're very lucky to have him."

"Aren't we, though? But, you know, he really loves reading the Bible until just that right illumination hits him. I'm sure he'll come up with something inspiring."

The next hour flew by as they chatted about logistics, setup and coordination while Becky remained happily absorbed in her new task. Pat disappeared into the kitchen and Gracie relaxed, experiencing that inner glow of satisfaction that meant a little progress had been made. Finally, Becky sighed and Gracie heard the familiar *calunk!* of the printer.

The young woman stood, picked up the paper, and stretched. "Is that coffee I smell? I'm dying for a cup."

"Your timing couldn't be better," Pat replied, returning with three steaming mugs on a tray. Just as she set them down, the phone rang. Answering it, Pat was immediately drawn into a lengthy conversation.

"Why don't we go outside?' Gracie suggested.

Becky nodded and, together, the two women sought shelter under a nearby apple tree. A soft breeze caressed their bare arms.

"*Mmm* . . . good. Perked coffee. You can always tell," Rebecca said, sipping with satisfaction. "Our office had one of those drip machines. The coffee's never hot enough for me."

"Pat's coffee is legendary. A real pick-me-up during those long budget meetings."

Gracie swallowed, then chuckled. "I know for a fact that this dark elixir has been the blessed tonic for many a frayed nerve, mine included."

Becky laughed lightly. "I couldn't have made it through school without it."

Gracie set her mug in a shallow depression between two tree roots. "I'm not sure I even know what you graduated in."

"Finance," Rebecca replied, her voice suddenly as flat as the church lawn.

"You didn't enjoy it?"

Becky frowned. "Honestly? Some of it was great. Very challenging. Really. But . . ."

"But what?" Gracie encouraged gently.

Coffee forgotten, Becky tugged loose a few strands of grass and dropped them in the breeze one by one. "I . . . I just didn't feel anything for the subject matter. But my dad kept telling me that it was essential for my career, that I should just buckle down and do it. He didn't understand. Difficulty wasn't the problem. I could handle the workload all right. It . . . oh, what's the use?"

Gracie's heart ached for her. "Why did you study finance?"

"I did it for my dad. He . . ." she tossed another blade of grass. "I know he wants what's best for me. And I've always wanted to please him. It didn't seem like such a bad idea at the beginning. I hate to admit it but . . . he was right. There are jobs in finance and banking. Good jobs. I've had several offers . . . he's *so* thrilled. That's really why I've come home for a few weeks. To try and decide."

She turned and stared into Gracie's eyes. For a moment, Gracie thought of Carter, her niece, and longed to be with her. She felt an urgent need to speak with her, to make sure she was safe. But Rebecca was talking.

"I go around and around in my head, but I always end up at the same spot. I don't feel anything for any of the offers, yet how can I disappoint my dad? It means so much to him." A single tear slipped down her cheek. "Do you understand, Mrs. Parks? It's just like college, all over again. I'm just going through the motions to please my father."

Gracie understood completely. On rare occasions, she and her late husband, Elmo, would drive to Chicago to attend a White Sox game. Elmo loved baseball, and, as he put it, there was nothing like the crack of the ball or the roar of the crowd on a hot summer night to make you feel alive.

Gracie thought watching professional sports was a waste of time, time better spent praying, singing or helping others. But she went along and was surprised to gain some very precious feelings: the gentle weight of Elmo's arm around her shoulders, the gleam of excitement in his eyes, the patience in his voice as he explained the play, those were the experiences she treasured that quickly made her cheer for the home team and thank God for these deepened moments.

Gracie took Becky's hand and squeezed. "Sometimes we do things for others and are rewarded in unexpected ways. Have you prayed for His guidance?"

"I've tried," Becky replied, "but my mind's such a jumble, I'm not sure I can hear Him." She turned away. "You see, there . . . there's another problem. My dad just . . ."she shook her head. "Oh, Mrs. Parks! I can't bear to disappoint him twice, but I don't know if I can live like this."

"Oh, dear. It can't be as bad as all that, surely? Have you spoken to your father? Your mother?"

Rebecca jumped up. "No! I . . . can't. Excuse me, Mrs. Parks but I'd better get back and see what else I can do."

"But . . . Becky, wait!"

She rushed off into the church. Gracie gathered their mugs and rose slowly. Life seemed so complicated, especially to the young. As she walked across the grass, she realized that it wasn't any easier as you aged, the years of seasoning only left you better equipped. She was thankful for every laugh line and aching joint earned from her sixty-two years of life, and for the resulting wisdom and opportunity to help others. *Dear Lord, I'm not sure what Becky needs right now, but I'll be there for her. I know You'd want that. Please give her the strength and courage to face and see beyond her fears. She's very special, and I know You have a wonderful plan for her.*

She stepped into the darkness of the sanctuary and listened for a moment. *I also know how mysterious Your ways are sometimes, but if You could give Becky a little sign, she would follow it to the ends of the earth to make You proud.*

PHEW! ANY MINUTE NOW, I'm going to dissolve into a puddle of pure jelly. Is anybody as hot as I am?" Estelle Livett asked, waving her sheet music in front of her face.

The others responded with a perfectly harmonized, "Yes!"

It was early Tuesday evening, and the members of the Eternal Hope choir were in the loft where barely a breeze crept in.

Barb Jennings, their director and accompanist, nodded and sagged over her organ keys. Marge hoisted her water bottle for the umpteenth time and greedily finished it. Gracie guiltily fantasized licking an ice cream cone.

Willow Bend's heat wave had continued over the weekend despite Uncle Miltie's firm belief that the weather was about to break. In fact, for the first time Gracie could remember, Pastor

Paul had eschewed his Sunday sermon, knowing that his flock was wilting and that the Lord would understand. Quickly reminding everyone of the upcoming Blessing Service, he took a moment to thank Rebecca Baxter for creating the flyer and to prompt the congregation members to take one or more as they left. Then, using several flyers as a fan, Paul waved them into the unrelenting sunshine.

This evening's practice for the Blessing Service had been erratic so far, what with Estelle's vigorous flapping, Marge's perpetual swallowing and Lester Twomley's ongoing efforts to keep perspiration from dripping onto his music. The choir's short but talented tenor had given up dabbing his forehead and had wrapped his oversized hankie around his head. Had she the energy, Gracie would have laughed.

"How about moving the practice outdoors?" Don asked. "I know we won't have the organ, but I think we could manage singing a cappella, don't you, Barb?"

"Great idea!" the Turner twins, back from their vacation, chimed, before Barb could reply. Though thirty-five and married, Tish Ball and Tyne Anderson would always be known as the Turner twins—and even their husbands accepted it.

"Well, if it'll help everyone's concentration. I'll bring my harmonica," Barb said, moving to the stairwell.

The others glanced around, then grabbed what they needed. Soon, they were strolling along the main sanctuary aisle toward the cool embrace of the shaded front steps.

"Ah!" Lester said, spreading his arms out. "Much better."

Barb blew sharply on the harmonica. She was confident and back to her usual no-nonsense self. "Okay, folks, let's get back in business." She glanced up.

"Good idea," she said, nodding at Lester, Don and Bert Benton, who had taken positions on the top stair. "The steps make a nice stage."

Rick Harding now picked himself off the lawn and dashed up to join his brothers in song.

"I really like this," Lester whispered into Gracie's ear. "I actually can see from up here."

Gracie grinned. In the crowded loft inside, Lester was forced to sit directly behind Estelle, whose ample size dwarfed him.

"Now," Barb said, taking command. "We're still undecided about our opening song. It's either 'For Every Creature' or 'God Who Touches the Earth with Beauty.'"

"I like 'For Every Creature,'" Don said. "It's a perfect opener. Those alleluias will get everyone into it, right off the bat."

Gracie wasn't surprised at Don's suggestion. His baritone voice frequently came in as a counterpoint to the soaring sopranos. In "For Every Creature," he and Bert had much larger roles, providing much of the *oomph!* to the chorus.

"I think we should open with the solo in 'God Who Touches the Earth,'" said Estelle.

Lester grimaced.

With their star soloist, Amy Cantrell, still on vacation, the role would go to Estelle, their second lead soprano. Gracie held her breath, waiting for the inevitable reference to the older soprano's experience. "That's how a professional choir would handle it. Wouldn't it, Rick?"

All eyes turned to the young African American. "Uh . . . well," he stammered, "that's certainly common, yes." He cleared his throat and gave Gracie a knowing glance. "Of . . . of course, I've heard it sung with a tenor solo. Makes for an interesting change." Rick Harding had had professional choir experience but preferred normally to play it down.

Estelle's face darkened, as though the stout woman had been suddenly thrust into deeper shadows.

Tyne Anderson kicked Gracie in the shin. Gracie muffled a laugh and twisted, so that Estelle wouldn't see. Below her, Marybeth Bower and Marge were burying their heads in sheet music.

"Why don't we call upon a show of hands?" Gracie suggested.

Barb nodded. "Okay, all those in favor of 'For Every Creature' raise your hand."

Every arm except Estelle's shot up in the air.

"That's settled then," Barb said. She looked up at Rick. "I like the idea of a tenor solo. What if we alternated, between you and Estelle, during the finale?"

"You mean, each of us sings a verse?" Estelle asked.

Barb nodded. "There are four in 'All Things Bright and Beautiful,' so two each."

"Great idea," Rick said. Don and Bert nodded. "As long as everyone else agrees."

"I can live with that," Lester replied. "We're all singing the refrain after each solo, right?"

"Exactly," Barb said. "So, are we all agreed?"

There was a murmur of agreement.

"Good. How about we give it a try then?" She played a note on the harmonica. "Let's begin with the refrain." She raised her baton and everyone stood at attention. "Together everyone!"

There was a collective breath as each choir member inhaled the warm evening air, and then the group began to sing. *"All things bright and beautiful, all creatures great and small. All things wise and wonderful, the Lord God made them all."*

Barb pointed to Estelle, who tackled the first verse. As her voice rose into the sky, a couple pushing a pram stopped and listened. Soon a small crowd dotted the front lawn. Little children tottered around their parents, while a pair of dogs wrestled enthusiastically.

As the group finished the last refrain and their voices slowly died, the audience jumped up and cheered.

"They love us!" Lester crowed. "Come on, Barb. Another one. Quick!"

But Barb Jennings was not to be rushed. It was a practice, after all. In the next half hour, she took her chorus meticulously through their paces, redoing and reworking sections as needed. The growing crowd didn't mind, clapping and whistling in appreciation.

A couple of minutes later, Pastor Paul Meyer pedaled slowly over the curve. With a grin, he pulled off his helmet and parked his bike. A couple of parishioners waved hello, and he warmly shook an elderly man's hand. For a while, he stood companionably with two baggy-jeaned teenaged boys.

As they waited for the men to finish their part in "God Who Touches the Earth with Beauty," Marge gestured in Gracie's direction. Pulling her eyes from a sandy-haired toddler, Gracie spied an official police sedan pulling into the parking lot.

Within seconds, Brooke and Emma Reynolds tumbled out, ice cream cones dripping in their hands. They were followed by a second set of twins. A moment later, Marybeth's husband, Chief Herb Bower, was assisting Uncle Miltie out of the passenger seat. The laughing group found an empty spot near a hedge.

As they settled down, Brooke and Emma waved and shouted, "Go, Aunt Marge!" "Yay, Mom!" yelled Corey and Casey Bower.

When they finished and the cheering ended, Barb thanked the crowd. Paul approached and shook her hand. He then reminded the audience to plan to attend the service. A few dogs happily chewed on the flyers he was distributing, as if they knew the invitations were including them.

"Thanks for the great suggestion, Don," Gracie said. "Singing outside is a whole different feeling, isn't it?"

He nodded.

"The acoustics may suffer," Estelle wisely noted, "but the audience involvement made up for that." She was beaming with pleasure.

"Don't forget to drop by my place Thursday night," Gracie called. After some discussion, she and her uncle had agreed to host a midsummer get-together, whether Carter came or not. Over the weekend, they had already extended a number of invitations. Several choir members waved in acknowledgment, while Marge excused herself to find her nieces.

As Gracie stood there, she realized how much better it would be to have the Blessing Service outdoors. That way, there would be no space restrictions and all breeds of animals could attend. *So this was why we practiced outside. It was Your idea, wasn't it?* Gracie glanced up at the church entrance and smiled, for the first time truly certain she'd been right to suggest the animal service. She asked Barb what she thought.

"Outdoors?" the choir director mused. *"Hmm.* Good idea. It sure went well tonight! But I guess it's up to Paul, isn't it?"

Gracie nodded, and, together, the women went in search of

their young pastor. Not surprisingly, they found him surrounded by parishioners. He caught Gracie's eye and excused himself.

"Boy, you guys outdid yourselves tonight!" he said, hugging them in turn. "The music came across just great. I don't know if you were concentrating too hard to notice, but you had the crowd in the palm of your hand. We all felt blessed, I think, to hear you."

"That's what we wanted to talk to you about. What do you think of holding the animal blessing outdoors?" Gracie held her breath.

"Well . . . I don't see why not. Sure would eliminate our space worries, wouldn't it?" His face seemed to light up from within.

Gracie smiled encouragingly.

Paul suddenly turned practical. "It occurs to me . . ." His brow was furrowed.

"What's wrong?" Barb asked him.

"Well, I don't mean to be negative," he began, "not when I like your idea so much . . . but . . . it'll take a bit of work to set up. We'll need some kind of raised platform, tables and chairs moved outside." He wiped his brow. "Unfortunately, now's the time of year when most folks aren't feeling too energetic. It might be hard to find enough help. For you, too, Gracie."

She bit her lip. "I'll ask around. I'm sure it'll be okay, that the right persom will turn up. We won't be having a fancy reception, just simple refreshments. That'll help a little."

"And what about letting people know?" Paul asked. "We just handed out a flyer saying to bring only house pets as we're holding the service indoors. Now we can accommodate a rhinocerous!"

Gracie and Barb exchanged a look. "We could have a phone blitz," Gracie offered. "I think Becky and a few others would help. The word would spread pretty fast!"

Barb nodded.

"You two are amazing!" Paul said. "Okay. I'm game to give it a try, if you are." The women smiled.

"So I'll ask for some extra pairs of hands in my prayers," Paul said.

"What's this about an extra pair of hands?" Uncle Miltie asked, slowly approaching.

"We were just talking about holding the Blessing Service outside," Gracie said.

Uncle Miltie glanced around. "Seems like a mighty fine idea. What's the problem?"

"There isn't any, really," Paul replied. "We're just short of help, that's all."

The elderly man cackled. "Your listeners sure enjoyed themselves tonight. That's all it takes. It's like a saying Gracie has on the fridge."

They all stared at Gracie.

A smile brightened her face. "'No church garden should be without turnips: turnip for meetings, turnip for service, turnip to help one another.'"

"That's right," Uncle Miltie said, throwing his arm around his niece's shoulder. "I've no doubt that help will turnip. Maybe not the full cavalry"—he grinned—"but enough so you won't be in a pickle!"

Gracie groaned.

So did everyone else.

7

HOW DID YOU and the twins hook up with the Bowers last night?" Gracie asked the next morning, buttering another slice of toasted multi-grain bread. It was just after eight-thirty, and she and her uncle were midway through their breakfast. Gooseberry had long finished his and was curled up on a nearby chair, exhausted from his morning prowl in the dew-covered grass. For the first time in weeks, the sky was cloudy, softening the impact of the rising sun. Of course, her uncle wasn't surprised, having expected the cool front for days.

He paused, cereal spoon dangling in mid-air. "Well, Brooke and Emma—they don't like to be called 'the twins,' by the way." Gracie raised her shoulders in surprise and gave him an I-didn't-know-that look. "Anyway, they were getting a little bored. I'd beaten them in Scrabble again, so I offered to buy them ice cream." He dipped his spoon, refilled, then popped it into his mouth. After a couple of seconds of chewing, he swallowed. "We walked down to the Sweet Shoppe, or I walked and they . . ." He chuckled. "They started singing and doing these crazy moves together, arms and legs all over the place. Emma called them dance routines, but if you ask me, they're a far cry from the fox trot."

Gracie laughed as she refilled their mugs with fresh coffee.

"We were just sitting outside eating our cones when Herb and the kids drove by. He stopped to say hello, and I introduced the girls. They were pretty amazed to meet the chief of police. Herb said they were just going to pick up Marybeth at choir practice and would Brooke and Emma like a ride in a police car?"

"Well, it was very kind of you to take them for ice cream. I know Marge—" She paused, interrupted by the doorbell. "Now, who could that be at this hour?" she asked, heading to the front door.

"Maybe it's Don again," her uncle's voice floated out to her. "I'll get out the eggs."

"Carter!" Gracie exclaimed, pulling open the door. Her twenty-eight year old niece stood on the step, a small suitcase at her side. "Come on in!" she said, throwing her arms around her. "It's Carter, Uncle Miltie!" she shouted.

"So I see," he said, arriving at her side.

"I hope you don't mind my showing up without notice," Carter said, hugging Uncle Miltie. "After giving your offer some thought, I realized I could use a little break from the city."

"Mind?" Gracie replied. "We're thrilled to have you, aren't we, Uncle Miltie?" He nodded enthusiastically. "You're always welcome here, you know that."

Carter pulled her suitcase inside and closed the door. "*Mmm*, that coffee sure smells good. Any chance there's enough for an extra cup?"

Soon Carter was sitting across from Uncle Miltie, sipping gratefully from a mug held in one hand while stroking a purring Gooseberry with the other. Gracie paused, taking the measure of her visitor in the morning light. Normally vibrant, spirited and healthy, Carter Stephens appeared thinner, with dark smudges underlining her eyes. Something was definitely troubling her. *Dear Lord, thank You for bringing Carter safely to us. I see now that she needs my help and I hope and pray that You will guide me to provide the necessary support. Amen.*

Gracie took a deep breath. "Carter, honey," she said, entering the kitchen, "how about a nice breakfast of bacon and eggs?"

Carter smiled faintly but shook her head. "I'm not very hungry, Aunt Gracie, but thanks for the offer."

"But you're skin and bones, girl!" Uncle Miltie exclaimed, squinting across at her. "What's happened to your appetite?"

"Is everything all right at work?" Gracie interjected.

"Everything's fine," Carter replied. "Really. It's just the heat. I haven't been very hungry, plus I've been doing quite a bit of running."

"Have you had anything to eat this morning?" Gracie asked, knowing her niece would have been up early. Had she stopped on the way?

Carter shook her head. Gooseberry stretched luxuriantly.

"How about something simple," Gracie offered, "like a slice of toast?"

Carter looked up. "Oh, all right. Thanks, Aunt Gracie."

Gracie busied herself slicing bread while Carter and her uncle chatted about the heat wave finally breaking.

"Another few days or so and I think it would have been a record," Uncle Miltie said. "I was re-reading my *Farmers' Almanac*. Claims this kind of dry spell isn't unheard of, but the last one was well over twenty years ago."

Gracie handed her niece a small plate holding a buttered slice of toast. Uncle Miltie pushed the peanut butter and homemade raspberry jam toward her.

"Tell us about your work," Gracie began. "I thought the courts might slow down during the summer."

Carter smiled faintly and shook her head. "That's why I love it in Chicago. Things run at top speed all year long." She took a tiny bite of toast and chewed without interest. "Actually, it has been a bit crazier than usual. We've had a rash of trial dates and a couple of the lawyers were on vacation, another off sick. They're all back now and it's under control, so I decided to accept your offer and have a little holiday."

Gracie reached out to pat her niece's hand. "We're so glad you did. How long can you stay?"

"At least until the service," she replied, the remainder of her toast left untouched. "I'm looking forward to some free time for training." She licked a smidgeon of peanut butter from her finger.

"What kind of training?" Gracie asked, exchanging a glance with her uncle.

"For a marathon. One of the guys in my office is a serious runner. He told me about this Marathon of Hope, to raise money for inner-city street kids. I've always wondered if I could run one and he's offered to help me train." She leaned back. "I really like it. The hard part's finding the time, but I've been walking, running a little . . . even cross-training on a bike. It's rigorous—but great for thinking."

"You're sure you're not overdoing it? You've lost weight—"

Carter jumped in. "I'm fine, Aunt Gracie. I'm in better shape now, that's all."

"Okay, dear," Gracie replied, clearly unconvinced. "I'm glad you're doing something other than work."

"You've come to the right place," Uncle Miltie said as he gently squeezed Carter's shoulder. "An infusion of our fresh

Indiana air, that's what you need. That and your aunt's home cooking." He nodded with satisfaction. "You'll be feeling like a new woman in no time."

Looking again at her niece, Gracie worried that it might take more than that to bring back the Carter Stephens she was used to seeing.

"GOOD AFTERNOON, LADIES!" Emma sang out as the overhead bell jangled and Gracie and Carter entered Marge's gift shop.

Interrupted while refilling a greeting card rack near the back, Brooke turned and smiled. Emma, meanwhile, was approaching to shake both their hands. "And how are we this afternoon?" she continued. "Well, I hope?"

"Very well, thank you," Gracie replied, playing her part.

Marge, seeing Carter, moved swiftly out to embrace her. Earlier, Gracie had suggested a stroll into town, a proposal to which Carter had quickly agreed. En route, Gracie had deliberately kept their conversation light, finding her niece preoccupied in any case.

Now Marge stood back and gestured. "Girls. I'd like you to meet Mrs. Parks's niece, Carter."

Brooke asked brightly, "Is there something in particular you were looking for, Mrs. Parks—or are you just browsing?"

Gracie couldn't bear it any longer. A giggle slipped free. "You two are wonderful!" She managed to gasp. She slowly gained control, swallowed and then said, "Oh, dear. Excuse me, girls, I didn't mean to laugh. It . . . it's just that you're both so polished, so professional."

"They're simply the best help I've ever had," Marge said, bursting with pride. "Natural saleswomen! Just like their aunt."

Everyone laughed.

It didn't take Gracie long, however, to realize that both girls soon were dazzled by Carter. Not surprising, she thought, as she watched them interact. Though a little pale, her niece couldn't help seem impressively sophisticated and capable. Marge, meanwhile, couldn't keep from boasting that Gracie's niece was not only a lawyer but Chicago's finest assistant district attorney.

That did it.

All thoughts of boosting their aunt's sales figures flew from their minds as they peppered Carter with questions.

"I'd be worried, too," Marge whispered, as she and Gracie moved behind the register.

Smiling at Carter, Gracie nodded.

"She's lost weight and doesn't look like she's been sleep—"

Gracie gently pressed her arm.

"Oh," Marge said. "Right." She raised her voice. "Now, girls, give the poor woman a chance! You're both talking to her at once."

Carter chuckled. "That's all right, Mrs. Lawrence. I'm recruiting for the DA's office."

"You really think I could be a lawyer?" Brooke asked.

Carter held her gaze. "Of course, you can. You can be anything." Her eyes moved across to Emma's face. "Both of you."

"I want to be an actress," Emma announced.

Carter chuckled. "You're what? Fourteen?" The girls nodded. "That's what I wanted to be when I was your age."

"But look at you now," Marge said. "You're a successful assistant district attorney."

"And I spend a lot of my time acting, don't I, Aunt Gracie?"

For a moment, Gracie froze, wondering if there was a deeper meaning to her niece's words. But she silently chided herself for looking for trouble, smiled and replied, "Oh, yes! I've seen Carter in court many times. She's terrific. A regular Perry Mason."

"Perry who?" Brooke asked.

Carter grinned. "Before your time. And he was a defense attorney, Aunt Gracie. Remember?"

The door bell jingled, and a trio of customers strolled in.

"Back to work," the twins whispered.

Carter held up her hands. "Duty calls. You'd better go."

"Can we talk again?" Brooke asked, as Emma approached the newcomers.

"I'd love to. I'm staying for a few days." She turned to Marge. "Bring them by sometime. If that's okay with you, Aunt Gracie?"

"Of course, dear," Gracie replied. "Why not dinner, tonight?"

Marge frowned. "Oh, I'd love to, Gracie, but it's not going to work. They're going to help with some inventory after I close."

"Okay, then . . . how about dropping by for dessert after you're finished? It'll give the girls something to look forward to."

"Great idea!" added Carter. "Aunt Gracie and I'll whip up something special."

As they said good-bye and strolled along the street, Gracie noticed Rebecca, accompanied by a young man, in a small crowd a couple of stores ahead. She waved and shouted out a hello.

Several faces, including Becky's, turned at the sound of her voice. She squinted, then grabbed her companion and pulled him into Robertson's Pharmacy. Embarrassed, Gracie dropped her arm to her side.

"Maybe she didn't know you were calling to her?" Carter said. "I'm sure she didn't mean to be rude."

Gracie nodded. "Maybe the sun was in her eyes." Then, playfully, she nudged her niece. "And just what *special* treat do you intend we whip up?"

Carter looked at her aunt in mock surprise. "Well, actually, Aunt Gracie, in the recruitment business, it takes one person to get the best candidates interested . . ."

"And . . . ?"

"The other closes the deal. Say, with a recipe for the best strawberry shortcake in town!" Laughing, she stepped off the curb.

A movement caught Gracie's eye and she shouted, instinctively grabbing Carter and yanking her back. Her niece tripped and tumbled to the sidewalk, just as a big motorbike rumbled by. It was a scratched and peeling vehicle—not some shiny new import—and its thick wheels just missed Carter's outstretched legs. Without stopping, it roared off.

"Oh, dear!" Gracie exclaimed, bending to her niece. Her heart pounded in her chest. "Carter! Are you all right? Oh, my sweet girl, you could have been killed!"

"I'm fine," Carter replied, wincing slightly. She grabbed Gracie's outstretched hand and pulled herself up. Gracie enveloped her in a hug and whispered a prayer of thanks.

"I'm all right," Carter said, her voice muffled by her aunt's embrace. "Honest." She gently disengaged herself.

"Not even a scratch." She held out her arms. "See? But, boy, that was close! Am I glad you were paying attention."

"That driver was a maniac! He almost ran you down and didn't even stop." Gracie was indignant. "The nerve! To think what might have happened!"

Now it was Carter's turn to provide comfort. She hugged her aunt tenderly. "It wasn't his fault," she said. "I didn't even look."

"Gracie! Gracie!" A deep voice shouted. A large man was approaching them, his expression panicky. "Are you all right?" asked the owner and editor of the *Mason County Gazette*.

"Oh, Rocky," Gracie replied, reaching to grab her friend's arm. "Carter was just nearly killed!"

"What?" shouted Rocky Gravino, his eyes suddenly wide. "Almost *killed*?"

"Everything's okay," Carter explained. "Nobody's hurt. I just walked into the street without looking. And almost got clipped by a speeding bike." She smiled affectionately at Gracie. "If it hadn't been for my aunt . . ."

Gracie shivered, despite the heat. Rocky noticed.

"You two should sit down for a while. You've had a terrible shock," he said. "Come on into Abe's and let me buy you a cool lemonade or iced coffee."

TEN MINUTES LATER, they were safely settled into a back booth at Abe's Deli. One look at Gracie's face when she'd come through the door had brought Abe Wasserman racing around the counter to assist her. Rocky quickly conveyed the details of the incident to him while Gracie and Carter sat down.

"Freshly made coffee cake, coming right up," Abe now said, heading back behind the counter.

Gracie's heart had returned to its normal rhythm and she reached for her glass of water, surprised by a sudden thirst.

"Feeling better?" Rocky asked, as Carter put her arm around her aunt's shoulder.

Gracie drained the glass, then gave a little "V" sign.

"Here we are," Abe said, carrying a loaded tray. "Help yourselves. It's on the house."

"Oh, no," Gracie started.

Abe held up his hand to forestall her protests. "Carter's been away far too long. That's all. It's both a welcome and a bribe to come back again soon."

"Oh, Abe, thank you!" Carter looked suddenly more like her old self in the warm reflected glow of Abe's obvious affection for her. Gracie and Rocky beamed as she reached for a piece of cake.

A few minutes ago, Gracie herself would have been incapable of eating; now she tackled Abe's cinnamon-pecan coffee cake with relish. She was pleased to see her niece doing the same.

Rocky watched Gracie happily. "Your appetite's okay. That's what I need to see. Gracie, my dear, I thought you were going to faint right onto the sidewalk."

Gracie sipped her coffee. Immediately, she felt a resurgence of indignation. "I guess I *am* myself again. But all I can think of is how I wish I could box the ears of that reckless driver!"

"What's going on here?" asked a man's voice.

The trio looked up. Fred Baxter had stopped at their table.

"Fred!" Gracie and Rocky exclaimed. "We're only celebrating a narrow escape and enjoying Abe's baking skills. Have a piece!"

"Hello, Carter," Fred said, extending a hand. "It's been a while. Everything under control in Chicago?"

She smiled at him.

Fred glanced down at the remaining cake. "How much of that is mine?"

"Just say when," Rocky said, reaching for the knife.

They told Fred what had just happened as he ate. He shook his head. "The good Lord be praised. I hope you gave proper thanks, Gracie. You two are surely blessed."

"That we are," she replied, squeezing her niece's hand. "By the way, I saw Becky the other day. She's looking very well."

"She's great, isn't she? Did you know she graduated top of her class?" He leaned across to Carter, confiding, "Might even give you a run for your money some day."

"Oh," she asked, "is she going to law school?"

"Not sure yet." He winked. "She might even follow the old man into banking. There are numerous offers, but she'll end up in finance or law. We know that for sure."

"Well," Carter replied. "Either one would make an interesting career."

"That's what I keep telling her," Fred said. "And head to Chicago, New York, San Francisco. . . ."

Carter looked at Gracie and Rocky.

"That's the life! The big cities are where it all happens." Fred sighed. "There sure isn't any high finance in Willow Bend. Being a mortgage banker's pretty small-time stuff."

"Now, come on!" Rocky objected. "We've got plenty of

excitement right here. Just last month, the Scouts raised over a thousand dollars for their summer camp." He cocked his head. "For most parents, that's pretty high finance."

"Okay, okay," Fred replied. "Don't think I don't love Willow Bend. . . ."

"But?" Gracie prompted.

"There's a great big world out there. And I want something bigger for my daughter than life in a small town." He dropped his voice. The others bent closer. "Besides, I'm hoping some distance and extra excitement will help change her feelings for her local swain. She has a romantic attachment to farming, in more ways than one."

"So she's still seeing Dennis McIver?" Gracie asked.

Fred frowned.

Rocky was curious. "You don't approve of the boy?"

An expression of exasperation now flooded Fred's face. "Don't get me wrong, Dennis is a good kid and treats Becky like a queen, even encourages her writing. Poems! Little cute essays about her feelings!" He snorted. "You wouldn't believe the stuff he's done to court her. Not just the usual flowers and candy, no siree.

"Last winter he took her for a midnight sleigh ride, and gave her a book of Elizabethan sonnets, I kid you not. Then, last Easter, he tried to give her a pair of lambs!"

Despite himself, he chuckled at the memory. "But . . . it doesn't matter . . . because he *wants* to be a farmer." Fred shook his head. "My Becky's loaded with talent. She could do anything. I don't want her settling on being some farmer's wife. I've foreclosed on too many families these last decades ever to let my daughter to go through something like that."

"Does she love him?" Carter asked softly.

Fred's eyebrows snapped up. "She can un-love him! It's her future I care about."

"I never gave my wife a pair of lambs, I'll tell you that," Rocky told them. "Chocolates maybe, but never sheep."

"You can't beat chocolates," Gracie said appreciatively. "Once, Elmo gave me a canary. He said it sang so beautifully, it reminded him of me." She glanced at Carter and was surprised at her niece's somber expression. Rocky, however, had a pleased expression on his face.

"When I was a teenager, I used to make frosted cupcakes for my next-door neighbor," Abe said, pulling up a chair. "She had long blond hair, same color as yours, Carter, and I was desperate for her to notice me."

"Did she?" Rocky asked.

"I'll say! She kept telling me how good they were and how wonderful I was. It took me weeks to realize that she was using my cupcakes to impress another guy!!"

They all laughed.

Suddenly, Carter slipped out of the booth and jumped up. "Excuse me," she said, "but I've got to go." She was gone before Gracie could say a single word. They stared at the door as it closed behind her.

"Gee, Gracie," Abe said. "I sure hope I didn't offend her."

Gracie was lost in thought. "Sorry, what did you just say?"

"What's wrong with her?" Fred asked, meanwhile.

Gracie replied, "I don't know. And I can't even guess." She sighed worriedly.

"Don't worry," Rocky said. "Maybe she was a little more shook up by her close call than she let on. She probably just needs a little time on her own."

"*Hmm*," Gracie replied, not convinced. "That's probably it."

She didn't fool anyone.

THANKS FOR THE LIFT," Gracie said as Rocky pulled up in front of her house.

"My pleasure, Ma'am."

"Want to come in?" she asked as they stepped onto her wide porch.

He glanced at his watch. "Better not." He gave her arm a squeeze. "Give my regards to Uncle Miltie. And tell Carter I hope everything's okay."

She waved as he sped away. Gooseberry suddenly appeared from behind the hydrangea bushes. With a long meow, he slunk up the steps and curled around her legs. She reached down and swept her palm against his soft back several times. He arched happily and began to purr.

"Are you okay?" her uncle asked, pushing open the door to join her.

"Is Carter home?" Gracie asked, interrupting.

He shook his head. "Something's bothering her. A while ago, she burst in the door and rushed off to her room. Barely said hello. A few minutes later, she was back, dressed in some tight shorts, telling me she's going for a bike ride."

They relaxed on the glider and Gooseberry leapt onto her lap. Gracie absent-mindedly scratched his ear as he curled into the crook of her arm.

"In a flash, she'd assembled a fancy bike out of pieces in her trunk and popped a helmet on her head. I asked her if everything was all right and she gave me a funny look. Then she smiled, more like herself, and hugged me. She said not to worry, that she just needed some exercise and would be back before dinner."

He glanced at his niece. "Something happen this afternoon?"

In the cool afternoon breeze, Gracie rocked while telling him the events of the day.

"Well, no wonder she was upset!" her uncle said, once Gracie got to the part about the motorbike. "A scare like that can really throw you!"

Gracie frowned. "It threw me, I can tell you! But Carter . . . Carter didn't get upset until later." Gracie told him about the conversation in the deli.

Uncle Miltie looked thoughtful. "So, Carter left Abe's just about the time you were talking about Abe's cupcakes? That is to say, gifts inspired by romantic feelings?"

Gracie told him, "That's right." Her cat stretched out a paw and prodded for more attention.

"That reminds me," Uncle Miltie said, rising. "Something was left inside the door earlier that must be for Carter. I want to show you."

Soon he had come back with a rectangular gold box embossed with the name of The Sweet Shoppe, Willow Bend's popular old-fashioned candy store. A small envelope was taped in one corner, but there was no name written on it.

She raised her eyebrows.

"Two pounds of their finest mixed chocolates. She ran out of here so fast, I didn't get the chance to give it to her."

Her uncle coughed. Gracie looked at him. His face flushed slightly as he handed the box to her. "Could be *personal*, you know. Man trouble."

Despite her worries about Carter, Gracie almost smiled at her uncle's old-fashioned term. She placed the box to one side, gently picked up Gooseberry and plopped him onto the porch. "I guess we'll just have to wait and see," she said.

Gracie had just finished peeling and dicing the potatoes for dinner when the phone rang. "Would you mind getting that?" she called to her uncle as she opened the oven door.

"It's for you," he said, poking his face into the kitchen. "Eleanor McIver, about the Blessing Service."

"Tell her I'll be with her in just one minute," Gracie replied, as she began to wipe her hands.

"Eleanor!" she said, picking up the phone "Everything okay?"

"Sorry to be calling so near dinnertime," the older woman replied. "I'm just waiting for my eggs to boil, and Ben's been pushing me to call to get the details on this Blessing Service straight. He tells me he heard that we can bring larger animals. Is that right? He wants to have a couple of heifers blessed. They're kind of runts. I told him he must be mistaken, that the inside of a church was no place for cattle. At least, not since the manger." She paused. "Don't laugh, but in addition to the dogs and cats, I was hoping to bring a favorite laying hen or two. They don't get much excitement." She chuckled.

Gracie settled back into the kitchen chair. "Ben's right. Paul and I were just discussing it the other night, and we decided we can hold the service on the front lawn. It's a bit of a late notice, but we were planning to do a phone blitz tomorrow to let everyone know. Just think of it like the Ark and bring a couple of everything!"

"Oh, Gracie, it will be wonderful! You know, sometimes I don't think we value God's creatures enough. And now we have a chance to make up for it."

"Well, credit goes to someone else. I'm just the person who was inspired by reading about it. By the way, how's Dennis doing? Don dropped by and told us about his gourmet produce."

Eleanor sighed. "Ben's fit to be tied and Jack . . . well, my eldest was never known for his patience."

"Don really seems to think it's an idea with a lot of potential."

"It may be, I just don't know. All I can say is that it's causing us a peck of trouble." She grew somber. "Ben's even rethinking his gift of land to the boy, says he's wasting good soil growing funny-colored lettuce and fancy vegetables only big-city folks have a taste for. I've told him not to be foolish, that he can't tell Dennis what to grow but . . . the McIvers are a stubborn bunch. I'm not ashamed to admit that it's a real problem in this family."

"I didn't realize there was so much disagreement. Have you spoken to Paul?"

"Not yet, but I've been praying for guidance."

"Why don't you give him a call? He might be able to help."

"I'll see, Gracie. I need to think some more. Now, before I go, is there anything I can do for you besides helping with the tables after the service?"

Gracie hesitated. She didn't like to take advantage, but in the past, Eleanor had always been a great assistant around the church kitchen, and occasionally in Gracie's part-time catering business. Gracie knew she couldn't count on Marge this time because of the girls. "Well, since we're having the service outside, Paul and I have agreed on some very simple catering ideas. Do you think you could take care of the juice and coffee?"

"I'd be happy to. Just let me know what the estimated numbers look like."

"I'll make sure there's more than enough on hand by the time you start setting up."

"You mentioned a phone blitz. I could start making some calls."

"Are you sure? I know you've got your hands full."

"I'm never too busy to help my church."

"Eleanor, you are a dear! I'll have Pat call you with names and numbers. How's that?"

Why aren't more of Your flock like Eleanor? she mused. *Why is it that most the church activities are put on with the willing spirit of the same dedicated people each and every year? Their lives are just as busy—if not more so—than the rest. Yet before you even ask, they think of giving, of helping others.* Gracie sighed. It seems it was ever thus. When Arlen was growing up, Gracie could have counted on one hand the number of parents who volunteered with her to drive and to coach, and to pitch in with fund-raising events like car washes and bake sales.

"Whatever is in that oven smells awfully good," Uncle Miltie said, clumping into the kitchen. "Anything I can do?"

Gracie put water on to boil and handed him a bowl of green and yellow beans. He sat and began breaking off the ends. "How's Eleanor?"

"Worried. Seems Dennis' farming is causing real friction in the family." She joined him at the table and grabbed a handful of beans.

They worked quietly for a couple of minutes, the silence broken only by the steady snapping.

Finally, Uncle Miltie spoke. "Have you heard about the string bean who rushed his friend, the pea, to the hospital?"

Gracie looked resigned.

"The string bean asks the doctor if he can save his friend's life." He broke a bean for emphasis. "The doc says that he has some good news and some bad news."

"*Umm?*" Gracie said dutifully.

Uncle Miltie cleared his throat. "The good news, the doctor says, is that he can save his life."

"What's the bad news?" a new voice asked.

There was Carter standing in the doorway, smiling. She rushed to the table and gave each a fierce hug. "Please forgive me! I'm so sorry. I shouldn't have run out like that on either of you."

"That's all right, dear. I'm just glad you're safe." Gracie had decided it would be better to give her niece the breathing space she needed. Hovering never helps, she wisely understood.

"So," Carter added, munching a yellow bean, "the doctor was saying?"

Uncle Miltie grinned. "He says the bad news is that his friend, the pea . . . would be a vegetable for the rest of his life!"

Carter laughed appreciatively, then suddenly stopped. "What's that?" she asked, pointing to the gold box.

"Oh!" Miltie replied. "I'm sorry, dear, I'm pretty certain it's yours. No one ever sends your aunt or me bonbons."

"Who's it from?"

Gracie and Uncle Miltie shook their heads. Uncle Miltie pulled off the tiny gift envelope and handed it to her.

Carter ripped it open, tugged the card free and stared. After a few moments, she closed her eyes.

"They're all yours, Uncle Miltie," she said, flipping the card onto the table. "I'm in training." She gave a thin smile. "I'd better go have a shower."

They silently watched her leave, then Miltie shook his head.

"That was a bit odd," he said. "I thought women loved to get chocolates."

"They do, normally," Gracie replied. She dragged the card across the table. "From your Secret Admirer," she read out loud. "I wonder who that could be?"

Uncle Miltie's fingers were already unfolding paper. "Whoever he is," he said, selecting a triangle wrapped in blue foil, "he's got great taste."

11

"H*MMM*, DEELISH!" Brooke Reynolds said, licking whipped cream off her fingers.

"I love strawberries!" her sister replied. There were short-cake crumbs and red stains all around their lips. Emma kicked her feet against the floor, shoving Gracie's old-fashioned glider into action.

Carter grinned from her perch on the porch railing. "This surely is a recruitment technique more corporations should employ. Forget paid vacations, pension plans and healthcare packages! Just promise them shortcake!"

Brooke peered at her half-eaten dessert, still puzzled. "Is it *all* strawberry?"

"Clever girl," Gracie told her. "I mixed in some homemade raspberry jam for an extra flavor boost."

Emma finished her glass of milk and sighed. "I wish my mom made desserts like this!"

"*Our* mom," her sister snapped.

"Duh," Emma drawled, shaking her head.

"Girls, *please*," begged Marge.

"Why not learn to make them yourselves?" Gracie asked. "You could surprise her."

"Do *you* cook?" Brooke asked Carter.

"Well . . . I like to. My job keeps me pretty busy, especially during the week," she admitted. "But sometimes, on the weekends, I have a bit of free time. Then I make several dishes and put them in the freezer. They'll last me the week. I find good food makes a big difference in my energy levels, especially now that I'm preparing for a marathon."

She smiled at Gracie. "Thank heavens for my aunt. She's taught me some great but simple recipes, so I eat pretty well. I'm just not a slave to my kitchen."

From her wicker chair near the door, Gracie smiled back, relieved by her niece's relaxed demeanor. Though Carter hadn't explained her earlier reactions—her flight from Abe's or her unease at seeing the box of chocolates—Gracie sensed in her niece a desire for openness. She could wait.

Brooke asked, "When did you know you wanted to be a lawyer?"

Carter grinned. "Almost from day one, I think. I took the cases of all my stuffed animals pro bono."

Gracie nodded. "My brother Buddy, Carter's father, used to tell a funny story."

"Oh, Aunt Gracie!" Carter protested, blushing slightly. "Not *that* one."

Gracie chuckled. "He said that there was a boy in Carter's first-grade class who was accused of stealing another boy's lunch."

"What'd she do?" Emma asked, leaning forward.

"She marched right up to the teacher and offered to defend him!"

Uncle Miltie slapped his knee and the girls howled with delight. Carter's blush deepened as her aunt and Marge joined in the laughter.

After a couple of minutes when everyone had settled down, Brooke quietly said, "I wish I knew what I wanted to be. It can be so confusing, when you think of all the choices."

"Do you know what you *don't* want to be?" asked Carter. "Sometimes it's easier to work backwards. You know, eliminate certain fields to help narrow your focus."

Brooke grimaced slightly. "I don't want to be an actress, like her."

"That's good," her sister replied, "because you'd be lousy. Besides," Emma added, flipping her arm dramatically, "*I* got all the creative talent."

"Did not."

"Did too."

"Girls!" Marge broke in. She hugged Brooke tightly.

"There's plenty of time, dear. Don't rush yourself. Enjoy being a teenager!"

"Your aunt's right," Gracie added. "Childhood and adolescence may seem confining, but they actually offer a kind of freedom you'll never know again."

"Darn tootin'!" Uncle Miltie raised his fist for emphasis. "Besides, the world is full of opportunities for bright young girls, like you two. Take our advice, explore it a little. I'm sure the good Lord will show you the way."

"Amen," Marge said.

Suddenly, a grinding roar assaulted their ears.

Carter jumped off the railing onto the front lawn and glanced down the street.

At that moment, a pumpkin-colored face poked under Gracie's post-and-split-rail front fence. Gooseberry wriggled under, then streaked across the lawn and flew up the steps.

"Oh dear!" Gracie exclaimed, as the quivering feline leapt onto her lap. Large smudges of black flattened the orange hair on his back. "Whatever have you been rolling in?" she said, staring at her darkened palm. "Oil?"

"Sounded like someone kick-starting a bike." Uncle Miltie cocked his head, listening. "You know—an old motorbike."

Just then, the deep roar rumbled right toward them. Gracie jumped up, unintentionally flipping her cat. He landed neatly on all four white paws as she charged down the steps.

A yellow motorcycle thundered into view. The bike slowed as it growled by the front of Gracie's house, its driver hidden behind a smoked shield and black helmet. Gracie shouted. "Wait a minute. Stop!"

But with a flick of the driver's wrist, the powerful engine belched, and bike and rider shot away.

THEY ALL RACED OUT onto Gracie's front lawn.

"What's the matter?" Marge asked, quickly approaching her best friend.

But Gracie was too surprised and frustrated to reply. Carter took her aunt by the arm and led her back to the porch and into her chair, as the others all sat back down again, one by one.

"It was just a noisy old bike, Mrs. Parks," Emma said.

Gracie nodded.

"There's more to it than that, Gracie, dear," Marge said. "You look like you've seen a ghost!"

"We had a bit of a fright earlier today, that's all," Carter began. "Let me explain." Quickly and concisely, as though addressing a jury, Carter related the incident. Gracie only interrupted once, when Carter explained that she had been at fault, stepping off the curb without paying attention.

"Maybe so," Gracie said, "but he was speeding! He should get a ticket, at the very least."

"The most important thing," Carter continued, "is that nobody was hurt."

"Are you sure it's the same bike?" Uncle Miltie asked.

The two women nodded. "It's pretty distinctive," said Carter. "That sound and the muddy yellow coloring."

Uncle Miltie nodded. "A Norton Commando. 750cc's." He whistled softly. "A real British classic. Nineteen seventy-one, seventy-two, maybe. Either way she's a beauty, even if it's in rough condition."

They all stared at him.

"How do you know that?" Brooke asked.

Uncle Miltie shrugged. "Same way a birdwatcher can spot a blue-throated hummingbird from forty paces. It's not the knowledge that carries the day, but the interest that gained you that knowledge in the first place. I happen to like machines, that's all, even ones that come close to running down my favorite nieces!"

"Tuska? Oh, Pigoletto's granddaughter!" Gracie laughed. "Of course, she's welcome, Mildred. That's great. See you Sunday," she said, punching the off button on her cell phone.

She leaned back in her chair, pulled a long list toward her and drew a heavy red line through Billingsly, just like she had done for all the names above.

It was mid-morning the next day and she was in her kitchen, along with Carter and Rebecca. Pat Allen had graciously divided the Eternal Hope membership index three ways, keeping a bunch for herself, assigning a smaller number to Eleanor, and giving the remainder to Gracie. In the past hour, the three women had slowly worked the list, informing the congregation—mostly by leaving messages on their answering machines—of the location change for the upcoming Blessing Service.

Given that they were over halfway through their task, Gracie calculated that they would be finished before lunch.

From across the kitchen table, her niece grinned at her and hung up Gracie's home phone. "Tuska?"

Gracie laughed. "A hefty little piglet. The granddaughter of Pigoletto, a prize-winning sow. Mildred Billingsly's son says she wants to be blessed."

"You're kidding!" Carter exclaimed.

"How does he know?" Becky asked, returning from the living room and flipping shut her cell phone.

"He asked Tuska, of course!" Uncle Miltie said, coming in the back door and hanging up his gardening gloves. "I've seen them walking in the park. That Billingsly kid treats the little porker like a dog. Even has its own lead, bright pink if you don't mind. He swears Tuska understands English. Pigs are very smart, you know." He slowly ambled to the counter. "Time for a break. You all sound like you could use a coffee."

"Love one," Carter said, "but I'll keep on dialing people until it's ready."

"Same here," Becky added, stepping into the hallway to redial.

Gracie stood and stretched. She then grabbed her crockery cookie jar, half-filled with snickerdoodles, and placed it on the table.

When the coffee was ready, Gracie called Becky in from the living room. Carter started pouring while Uncle Miltie headed for the fridge.

"Mrs. Larson—whose son is bringing two goldfish, by the way—reminded me that you had some unwelcome excitement yesterday," Becky said. "I'd totally forgotten. My dad mentioned something about it as well."

"Jessica?" Gracie raised her eyebrows, not really surprised that the chairperson of the Eternal Hope Board of Directors knew about Carter's near-accident. Nothing remained secret very long in Willow Bend. Some people might be disturbed by the efficiency of her small town's grapevine but, for the most part, Gracie saw its value. Big city advocates could puff out their chests, railing against the lack of privacy and the prevalence of gossip in communities the size of Willow Bend. Not Gracie Lynn Parks. She would take a nosy neighbor over an indifferent one any day of the week. She liked to feel that others were keeping an eye out for her in the same way that she watched over them. After all, God said, "Love thy neighbor." Well, you sure can't do that if you won't even take the time to introduce yourself and make an effort to learn their names.

Rebecca nodded. "Her husband Ed was in town when it happened. He said some guy on a huge motorbike practically ran Carter down." She took a mug from Carter, then asked, "Is it true?"

Carter sighed and plunked down onto her chair. "Not exactly." She took a cautious sip. "I stepped off the curb without looking. End of story."

Gracie started to speak, then thought better of it. Maybe her niece was right. Had she jumped to the wrong conclusion? It wouldn't be the first time she'd been blinded by her emotions, especially when it came to her loved ones.

"Have you decided on a career?" Carter asked Rebecca. "Your dad was telling us about some of your job possibilities yesterday."

Becky took her time before answering. "Not yet. I'd like to keep my options open."

"Are they all in Chicago?"

"No. One's with a bank in New York, another's with a brokerage firm in Pittsburgh."

"Nice to have options," Carter said, nodding approvingly.

"Do the companies vying for you know there's competition, or are you just dealing with them one on one?"

"One on one for now. Why?"

Carter smiled. "Well, if you found more than one job interesting, you could play them against one another. You know, barter for a better deal. If not for more money, then for perks. Parking, stock options, that sort of thing. The best time for negotiating is before you accept. Take your time, make sure the job and the company are everything you want or will help you to get what you want. Once you're in, you can find yourself locked in a position and it can get a lot harder."

She hesitated, drumming the table. "On the other hand, it's pretty common these days for people to have three or four careers in a lifetime. Sometimes one thing will lead to another. Find something that excites you and you'll do well. It's just human nature."

"You seem to know an awful lot about it," Gracie said, eyeing her niece in a slightly new light. "Is that what you did?"

Carter chuckled and swirled her coffee. "Working in the DA's office isn't quite the same as in a private bank or law firm, Aunt Gracie. We don't have huge salaries or very many perks."

Becky leaned forward. "Do you like working there?"

"Absolutely! You see, I knew from the first year of law school that I was more interested in service than in making money or headlines." Carter's eyes shone. "I love what I do. I handle a variety of cases, oddly enough, many with high profiles. Of course, we're short-staffed, under tremendous public pressure and running from docket to docket, but you know? I wouldn't want it any other way. In the DA's office, I get to tackle all the challenging issues I want—possibly a lot sooner than if I were acting for the defense—and, for the most part, I'm able to live with the results." She raked her fingers through her hair. "Occasionally, I'm up against one of my law school buddies. I'm not too sure that they can always say the same. I know I sleep better."

"Must be wonderful to do what you love. It's obvious you're good at it." Becky looked thoughtful.

"She's brilliant!" Gracie exclaimed. "Isn't she, Uncle Miltie? And we're not prejudiced!"

Uncle Miltie nodded vehemently. "Best in the city. We've seen Carter in action many times. A lot of the procedures are over my head, but Carter has a way with juries. She can take the most complicated bits of information and somehow convey them clearly. They love her. You can see it in their faces."

Carter flushed slightly. "Well, I'm not so sure about that," she replied humbly. "But I try to do my best. Fortunately, it's not so hard to when you're fighting for what you believe in." She grinned.

"Besides, on the days when everything blows up on me, I'm not far from two of my best friends and the tastiest home cooking anywhere!" She smiled warmly at her relatives. "But seriously, Becky, don't overestimate how nice it is to be close to family. Every job has its drawbacks, but they're easier to handle with a little help. As you can see, I get spoiled here."

Gracie placed her hand over her niece's. "And we love doing it."

Uncle Miltie nodded. "Guess you'd rather stick with Chicago, too, Becky?" he said. "Closer to home."

Carter said, "I really recommend it. It's a great town."

"Yeah," Becky replied slowly. "I guess so." She didn't seem convinced.

The others glanced quickly at one another.

"Somewhere else you'd rather live, Becky?" Gracie asked.

Instead of answering, the young woman stood. "Better get back to our job, if we want to finish by lunch. Thanks for the coffee, Uncle Miltie."

"Okay, back to the trenches," Carter said.

"Before you pick up the phone," Gracie started. She hesitated, praying that what she was going to say would please her niece. "Carter, dear, I hope you don't mind but Uncle Miltie and I have arranged a bit of a party for tomorrow evening. We were planning it as a surprise, but now I think it's better you know."

To Gracie's relief, Carter's face lit up. "That's very kind of you, Aunt Gracie! Yes, I'd love a chance to see some of your friends."

"Good," Gracie replied. "We're doing it outside, so it will be pretty casual."

"I'm organizing another game of croquet," Uncle Miltie said. "It was such fun last year. Remember?"

"Oh," Carter said, her voice dropping ominously. "Only on one condition."

Uncle Miltie looked worried. Gracie held her breath.

"That I'm on *your* team. Last year, I seem to recall I spent most of the game watching you smack my ball into Mrs. Finkmeyer's hedge!"

13

THE DOORBELL RANG. Gracie hesitated, caught in the action of pouring a bottle of ginger ale into her large punch bowl. She automatically glanced outside, and was immediately pleased with what she saw. The late afternoon rays of sun, softened by a light curtain of wispy clouds, bounced off the colorful cloth that draped a long table on her porch. In several vases were bouquets overflowing with Gracie's own perennials. The white spiral hoops that Uncle Miltie used to outline his croquet course dotted the front lawn.

With her uncle and niece's help, all of the necessary chores had long been completed. Along with the table, her wide, front porch now boasted a row of her dining chairs, as well as additional deck chairs borrowed from Marge. The punch glasses were laid out, the cheese, cracker and liver pâté platter was ready, and the olive pinwheels were chilling in the fridge. Dessert was simple: coffee, tea and lemon squares with a graham cracker crust. There were also bowls of tasty salted cashews dotted around.

"I'll get it," Carter said, putting down the coffee pot. "Somebody always comes early. You finish mixing."

Gracie nodded, emptied the second bottle, added ice cubes and reached for more orange juice. She was glad she had dressed early and felt comfortable and cool in her soft cotton blouse and dark Capri slacks. She admired her niece's simple linen sheath but herself had abandoned short skirts many years ago.

"What are you making?" her uncle asked, from his hunched position at the kitchen table. Pen in hand, he had a pile of paper slips on his left and a small ceramic bowl on his right.

Gracie smiled. "It's called a 'bowl of sunshine.' Equal parts orange juice and ginger ale. Want a taste?" She filled a ladle, poured the contents into a punch glass and handed it to her uncle. "It's a slight variation on the usual mix. I know you'll like it."

He sipped, then eagerly swallowed the rest. "Hey, that's mighty refreshing! Just the ticket for our croquet players. Oh, by the way, is Rebecca Baxter bringing anyone?" he asked, writing the young woman's name on a slip of paper.

"*Hmm*," Gracie replied, slicing an orange. "I don't think so. When I mentioned the party, she was very excited. Sadly, she looked less pleased when I asked her to invite her parents."

Uncle Miltie shrugged. "Oh, well," he said, dropping the slip of paper into the bowl to join the others. He reached in to stir them. "I can always add another name."

"Oh, *no*," a strangled cry came from the front door.

"Carter?"

A soft moan was the only response.

Gracie dropped the knife and raced into the hall. "Carter, what's wrong?"

Her niece leaned shakily against the door. A huge bouquet of roses hung upside down from her hand.

"Not again!" Carter was saying, shaking her head. "Not here. Why does it keep happening?"

"What are you talking about, dear?" Gracie asked, slowly approaching. "I don't understand."

Carter's lovely face turned to stone. "It's nothing," she replied, striding past her aunt.

Gracie followed her into the kitchen where she saw Carter dump the flowers into the garbage bin!

"But—"

"Hey! What're you—" Uncle Miltie started.

"Please! Aunt Gracie, Uncle Miltie," Carter spat out hurriedly, "please, for my sake, just leave them, okay?" Her intelligent eyes darkened. "I can't talk about it right now, but I beg of you. Just leave them."

Before Gracie could answer, the front door bell rang again.

As though glad to be out of the kitchen, Carter turned on her heel and headed to the hallway.

Uncle Miltie walked over and peered into the garbage. "These are beautiful!" he said, prodding the cellophane that covered the long-stemmed yellow roses. "Somebody's sure sweet on Carter." He gently tugged free the envelope holding the card. "Any idea what's going on?"

"None, but I want to respect Carter's wishes. Agreed?"

Her uncle pulled his hand back as though burned. "Sure," he said, stuffing the envelope into his shirt pocket as excited voices slipped in from the hall.

A moment later, the Turner twins' identical cheery faces poked into the kitchen. Wearing matching baby-blue sundresses and floppy yellow hats, they stood in front of their husbands, Bill Anderson and John Ball, who were dressed in shorts and golf shirts.

"We're on the same team, right?" the twins asked Uncle Miltie.

"Now, girls," he replied, with a wink, "you know the drill from last year." He scooped up the remaining slips of paper, stuffed them into the bowl and handed it to Bill Anderson. He stuck a wide-brimmed straw hat on his head. "Come on out to the front yard. You can get some practice in before the others arrive."

As the group trooped down the hall, Gracie reached for the punch bowl.

"Here, let me help you," Rocky said, entering the kitchen. "A lovely lady like you shouldn't be carrying anything so heavy."

"Thank you, sir," she replied, picking up the cheese platter and leading him down the hall and onto the porch.

She was surprised to find a crowd already gathered. She smiled as Fred Baxter and his wife mounted the steps. In a corner, Don was chatting with Becky and Carter, who'd regained her composure. For a moment, Gracie wondered if Don was the secret admirer who had sent the chocolates. He had always been sweet on her niece. But surely he wouldn't have also sent the flowers? Gracie temporarily shrugged off such minor mysteries and joined her guests.

Nearby, seated around a small table, Brooke and Emma were entertaining the Bower children. A small knot of people, a couple of them wielding croquet mallets, crowded around her uncle on the lawn. Tish and Tyne, sharing a mallet, were near the fence concentrating on lining up a bright red ball with the starting wicket. Suddenly, Gooseberry appeared from the hedge and marched over to butt the ball out of position.

"Hey," the identical women exclaimed. "No fair!"

"Hope you don't mind, Gracie," Lester Twomley called from the glider. Estelle and Barb waved from their seats beside him. "We were going to ring the doorbell, but everyone was already out here."

"Don't be silly," she replied, making room on the table for the punch bowl and platter. She raised her voice while pouring a glass and handing it to Rocky. "Punch anyone?"

Though he looked rather conservatively casual from the ankles up—dressed in a navy polo shirt and pressed chinos— Gracie was amused to see her old friend sporting sandals. "Same rules as last year?" he asked, while Lester filled glasses and started handing them round.

Lester chuckled. "Didn't think we had any?" He glanced down at the group around Uncle Miltie. "Have they picked the teams?"

"I think Uncle Miltie's got it all rigged, anyway," Gracie laughed.

It only took a couple of minutes for her to slice and arrange the pinwheel sandwiches and pickle bowl on a platter and return, but as she stepped onto the deck, her uncle was finishing announcing what he grandly called Uncle Miltie's House Rules.

"Okay, folks, last but definitely not least, is the famous . . ." He paused.

"Uncle Miltie's Rule of Thumb," a number of guests droned. Everyone chuckled.

"That's right! As sole judge and arbiter of any disputed plays in this contest, my gesture—thumbs up or thumbs down—is final."

"Let's pick the teams," Rick Harding shouted from the kitchen window where he had gone to get a cheese knife, "before it gets dark."

There was a round of applause after which Uncle Miltie gravely held the ceramic bowl in front of Gracie. "Oh, I almost forgot," he added, spying Gooseberry sprawled in the middle of the lawn. "Gracie's cat, the celebrated Gooseberry, is part of the course. You hit him, you start over, but any ball he moves remains in play."

Lester started a chant, "Gooseberry! Gooseberry! Gooseberry!"

Uncle Miltie shot him a look and continued, "This year, we've decided to name the teams in honor of our local churches."

Gracie pulled out the first slip. "Marybeth, captain of the Waxmire Tabs!"

The police chief's wife came forward.

Gracie read the next paper, "Fred, you're captain for the Trinities."

The banker chuckled and joined Marybeth.

Gracie quickly removed and read the rest of the names until all four teams were chosen.

Soon, croquet mallets were slicing the air sending colorful balls skipping and snaking across the lawn, accompanied by groans or cheers. While two teams played, the others leaned over the railing, shouting advice or hooting at the many mis-hits. Lester, hitting third for the Evangelos, spent much of his free time digging balls out of Hallie Finkmeyer's hedge. By fluke or heavenly design, Gracie hadn't decided, Don and Carter landed together on the Hopesters. She was delighted to see the young pair laughing and good-naturedly plotting strategy with Estelle, their lead striker. The get-together *had* been a good idea.

"This is a great party," Rocky said, smiling even though his own team had lost in the first round. He dropped onto the glider beside Gracie and handed her a punch refill. "I haven't had so much fun since I got to dunk Herb at last year's county fair."

Gracie laughed, recalling the startled look on the police chief's face when the ball thrown by Rocky hit the lever and Herb began dropping into the water tank. "If I recall, you hit it on the first pitch."

He nodded, then downed his punch in one gulp. "The extent of my prowess. My croquet ball ended up in your neighbor's hedge half the time. Hallie should charge us to reclaim them. She'd be rich!"

"Yeah," Lester added, joining them on the glider. "No wonder we lost."

"Nice flowers," Rocky said, gesturing toward the table. "Pretty professional looking."

Gracie shook her head. "All from my garden."

"Did you ge—"

There was a cheer. They glanced down to see Don, Carter, Susan Baxter and Marge—who Gracie thought looked particularly smart in a new denim shirtwaist—exchanging high fives. "Eternal Hope swings!" Don shouted, then joined the others shaking hands with the losers.

"Tough loss," Rocky said, as Paul Meyer bounded up the steps.

The young pastor grinned. "Behold, I have played the fool, and have erred exceedingly."

"Joshua?" Gracie asked.

Paul shook his head. "Saul." He rubbed his hands. "At least, this means we can move on to dessert."

14

SOMEONE'S BRINGING a *pig* to our Blessing Service?" Marge asked, reaching for another lemon square.

The sun sank in the sky, staining it crimson. A soft breeze cooled the air, causing many of the guests to pull on a sweatshirt or jacket. Short squeals of delight drifted up from the lawn where Brooke and Emma played a less cutthroat game of croquet with the Bower children. Gracie's adult guests were scattered in small groups along her porch, some sipping tea, others savoring her strong coffee. After a lengthy, hotly disputed minute-by-minute rehash of every play of the croquet tournament and a half-hearted attempt by the younger men to juggle the red, yellow and blue balls, talk had finally turned to other matters.

"Piglet, really," Gracie replied, savoring the last crumbs of her lemon square. Gooseberry was dozing on her lap.

"A pig-squeak," Rick Harding added, tickling his young daughter, Lillian.

Several guests laughed.

"This is going to be great fun!" Lester said, shifting his position on the railing. "I hear the whole McIver family's coming." He grinned. "That includes two dogs, three cats, a couple of calves, a billy goat and some hens."

"Family nothing," Uncle Miltie replied, with a chuckle. "Sounds more like their entire barnyard!"

"Hey, Becky," Rick called. The young woman looked up with a smile. "What's Dennis going to bring?"

Of course, thought Gracie. That had been the young man she'd seen her with in town!

Don joked, "Well, he's growing lamb's lettuce!"

"Ha!" Lester said. "That's a good one. Does every head come with a sheep?"

Rebecca glanced quickly at her father, then lowered her eyes.

"What's lamb's lettuce?" Estelle asked.

"It's also called mâche," Don replied. "Tangy, nutty greens. One of Dennis's best sellers."

"Oh, yes, those *designer* vegetables." Estelle yawned. "Who needs them? Honestly, Rebecca, I don't understand what your boyfriend thinks is wrong with good old-fashioned iceberg."

The young woman flushed.

"Becky wouldn't know if Dennis McIver's even coming to the Blessing Service," Fred Baxter said. "Right, honey?"

His daughter looked miserable.

"Of course, he's coming," Don replied. "All those wonderful new tastes. Some of you should try them before condemning them, don't you think?"

In the fading light, it was suddenly uncomfortably quiet. Then Paul's voice rang out, reassuringly. "Everyone's welcome," he said. "Everyone. And all creatures, too." He reached for his bike helmet and approached Gracie. "Well, it's getting dark, so I'd better be off. Thank you for a wonderful evening!"

Rick and his wife also rose. "Guess we'd better go, too," he said, his eye on his daughter sleeping in his arms.

Others stood, stretching. They began thanking their hostess and in pairs or groups of three, they slowly drifted off, chatting softly as they crossed the yard. Soon, only a few remained, offering to help with the cleanup.

"Where do you want these?" Don asked, hoisting a stack of matching deck chairs.

"Oh," Marge said. "Those are mine. Could you put them on my porch next door?" She nodded to her nieces. "Would you mind grabbing those plates and taking them inside?"

"Hey, Don," Lester called, returning from the kitchen, "let me give you a hand."

"You ever tasted lamb's lettuce?" Rocky asked, following

Gracie a couple of minutes later into the kitchen, a tray of mugs in his hands. They joined Marge at the kitchen sink.

Gracie shook her head and started to dry the dishes.

"Me neither," he replied, grabbing a dish towel. He glanced quickly around and lowered his voice. "Never thought I'd say this, but I'm with Estelle on this one. Crunchy iceberg's more my speed."

"What?" Gracie said. "You, the investigative reporter, afraid of a strange green leaf?" She looked at him challengingly. "I haven't tried much myself, but, you know? Don's right. People *are* reluctant to try new things. I'm sure if we had a taste, we'd find we liked them."

"Liked what?" her uncle asked.

"Dennis's new and improved farm produce."

Uncle Miltie shuddered. "Any day now, I expect Gracie to start serving dandelions."

"Makes great wine," Don Delano said, appearing at the doorway, along with Carter and Lester. "Or so they say."

"Eeeowww!" the girls moaned. Emma added, "They're weeds. That's *totally* gross."

"Anything else, Gracie?" Don asked.

She glanced around then shook her head. "No, it's all under control. Thanks. Carter, why don't you show them out? We can finish up here."

"If you're sure, Aunt Gracie."

"Oh, before you go," Uncle Miltie quickly began. "Somebody sent my great niece a box of chocolates. Either of you two know anything about it?"

Lester frowned. Don opened his mouth. "Wasn't there a card?"

"Chocolates?" Emma cried. "Somebody sent you chocolates?"

Brooke sighed, "How romantic!"

"No, Uncle Miltie, I'd really rather . . ." Carter started then stopped. *"Please."*

Gracie shot her uncle with a *not now!* look as her niece quietly said good night and climbed the stairs to her bedroom.

"Come on, Lester," Don said. "We'd better go. Thanks again, Gracie."

"Guess I'm the only one left," Rocky began, reaching across to toss a crushed napkin into the garbage. "Better get out of your . . ." He stiffened upon seeing the bouquet, and shoved the napkin in his pocket. "Good night and thanks," he said abruptly.

Before she could reply, he had opened the screen door and disappeared into the dark. When the door slapped shut, Gracie almost felt as though she had been struck.

"What are you staring at?" her uncle asked a minute later, dropping heavily onto a kitchen chair.

"Huh? Oh . . . nothing."

"I'm rightly tuckered out. That was some party."

"You can say that again," Gracie replied, her mind buzzing with questions.

"HERE," UNCLE MILTIE SAID, shoving the gold box across to his niece. "Try the square one with the wiggle on top. Nougat and caramel." He smacked his lips.

It was almost 10:00 P.M. and they were sitting congenially on the porch, enjoying the night stillness and the silvery gleam of a new moon overhead. Gracie remembered the many wonderful evenings she and Elmo had spent, chatting and swaying on the glider. Somehow their problems seemed smaller and more manageable after exposure to fresh air, sensible discussion and the odd prayer or two.

She pushed back and let the chair rock. What would El have said or done about Carter if he were sitting beside her? She waited, letting an image of her dear husband and the sound of his deep voice fill her mind until she could almost feel the pressure of his hand on hers. *Be patient, honey, and wait. Folks usually talk when they're ready and not before. Pushing them just makes things worse.*

Something rustled down on the lawn. Two tiny silver spheres appeared and blinked, as Gracie's cat slipped into the moonlight. After a quick glance in the direction of his humans, Gooseberry trotted across the grass and wiggled under the railing, leaving a glistening dark trail in the dew.

With a sigh, Gracie pushed forward on the glider and glanced down at the box of chocolates. For once, the lure of chocolate held no appeal. "No, thanks." She could sense her uncle's concern but didn't know what to say. "I guess I ate too much earlier," she added, trying to soften her lack of enthusiasm.

"Do you mind if I have one?"

Gracie and her uncle turned at the sound of Carter's voice. The young woman stood in the doorway, her silhouette framed in yellow light.

"Of course!" Gracie exclaimed. She patted the empty seat beside her. "Come and sit here, dear."

As Carter settled beside Gracie, Uncle Miltie presented the box. "That one. With the squiggle," he said, jabbing with a gnarled finger. "It's really good." Then, as though realizing for the first time how many he'd eaten, he added sheepishly, "I saved you the best ones."

Carter reached in and popped the chocolate into her mouth. After a moment of chewing, she nodded. "You sure did, Uncle Miltie. Thanks." She inhaled deeply. "It's beautiful out here. I love Chicago, don't get me wrong, but this is a

great place to escape to. And the company's not bad, either."
She took another breath. "The air's so fresh, it's purely
delicious."

Her heart suddenly lighter, Gracie threw an arm around
the young woman's neck and hugged her. "I'm so glad
you're here."

"Me, too, Aunt Gracie," she replied, hugging back. "I'm
sorry I've been acting a little oddly." Carter sighed. "It . . . it's
just . . ."

Gracie waited a moment then softly said, "Whatever it is,
we love you and are here for you." *Should I push, dear Lord? Is
she asking me for help or for patience?*

Uncle Miltie laid a comforting hand on Carter's arm.

"I know, and I'm grateful, believe me."

"Something's troubling you, dear," Gracie said, suddenly
confident in her words. "Would you like to talk about it?
Sometimes it can help."

Carter pursed her lips. "It's really a silly thing, but I guess
I've let it get to me." She looked each of them squarely in the
eye, then glanced away. "You know how something can bug
you but it doesn't get out of hand unless *you* let it?"

Gracie nodded. "Uh huh," Uncle Miltie said. "Couple of
my pinochle buddies spring to mind."

The young woman released an explosive sigh. "Well, I've
let this little problem—and compared to the cases I deal with
every day, it's almost a joke—but I've let it get to me. And

now . . . oh, it's just so stupid!" She ran her fingers through her hair. "That's why it's so hard to talk about—because it's my own fault."

Gracie almost spoke but she heard Elmo's voice whispering in her ear. *No, honey. Not yet. Give the girl some time. Just wait for it. She's ready, she wants to talk. Just let her be and she'll tell you everything.* She glanced at her uncle and saw that he, too, was holding his breath.

They sat quietly for several minutes. Finally, Carter spoke. "This is so embarrassing." Gracie squeezed her shoulder. "Okay. Don't laugh, but I'm being pursued by a stranger." Carter gulped. "A secret admirer."

Uncle Miltie gaped.

"A . . . a what?" Gracie asked.

"I know it sounds trivial, but someone's been sending me notes, flowers . . ." she pointed to the chocolate box. "Candy. It's been going on for weeks. And just before I came, he left a phone message on my home answering machine. That really freaked me out." The young woman looked up. "But now, it doesn't seem very threatening, does it?" Her expression was sheepish.

Gracie exclaimed, "Carter, honey! Of course, it does! My goodness, some crazy man is stalking you!"

"So that's why you threw out the flowers and refused the candy!" Uncle Miltie grabbed his cane and crushed it with both hands. "Boy, I'd sure like to get my mitts on that little creep. What did he say on the phone?"

Carter thought a moment. "The same stuff he's been saying in his notes. That he loves me. That he wants to be with me. That only *he* can make me happy. It . . . it was his *tone* that was a bit scary. Verging on anger. I've got to admit, you guys, I'm a little worried his actions might escalate into something violent. He's definitely getting frustrated."

"Have you told the police?" Gracie asked.

Carter nodded. "Not at first. At first, it was kind of fun, you know? It sounds ridiculous, but I was even flattered. I've been working too hard lately and haven't . . . well . . ." She lowered her eyes. "I haven't had much time for dates. I just thought it was probably one of the guys at work. But when the flowers and candy kept coming, I told them that enough was enough. And each and every one of them swore they had nothing to do with it. I asked all my friends, everyone I could think of—but no one's admitted responsibility."

"You believe them?" Uncle Miltie asked.

The young woman smiled slightly. "I make my living deciding whether people are telling the truth or not."

Uncle Miltie glanced at Gracie. "Is it possible it's someone you had been seeing, dear?" Gracie asked gently. "Someone *you* broke up with?"

"I don't think so, Aunt Gracie. I haven't seen anyone

seriously in a long while. As I said, I've been too busy to even date."

"What are the police doing about it?" Uncle Miltie asked.

"There's not much they can do, really. Someone's sending me presents, following me, but no real crime's been committed."

"Not ye—" Uncle Miltie caught himself.

Gracie repeated slowly. "Someone's following you . . ."

Carter nodded. "Has to be. He even knew I was here to send the flowers and candy."

"Oh, dear me," Gracie whispered.

"The motorcyclist!" she and her uncle exclaimed simultaneously.

"The motorcyclist?" Carter asked.

Her relatives nodded vehemently. Uncle Miltie said, "That's it! He's been nosing around ever since you came, hasn't he, Gracie?"

"Why, he even tried to run you down!" Gracie exclaimed. "He *is* dangerous!"

"Wait a second, Aunt Gracie. That was my fault," Carter replied. "Remember?"

But her aunt was on her feet. "He rode right by the front of our house. The nerve! It's him, Carter. I know it. And we're not going to wait around until he hurts you."

"No sir," her uncle added.

"Maybe the Chicago police don't take this very seriously, but I know Herb Bower will."

Uncle Miltie's expression was grave. "Come on, let's go in. You never know who's out there."

Gracie shivered. Suddenly, her pleasure and comfort with the darkness changed into fear and anxiety. As she followed the two inside, she turned and prayed silently. *Dear Lord, thank You for this wonderful evening of friendship and affection. I know I am blessed by, and am grateful for, Your guardianship and support. Please help me now to protect my dear niece. There is a man somewhere out there who's ill and I'm sure could use Your help. There must be a way to discover his identity and provide him the care he needs before it's too late.* Gracie felt a surge of confidence. *No one's going to harm my niece. Not if You and I can help it!*

LOOK, I'M REALLY SORRY, GRACIE," Herb Bower said, "but my hands are tied. Your niece is right. I know it sounds crazy, but the guy sending her presents hasn't done anything criminal."

"Yet," Gracie replied, her confidence from last night faltering in the mid-morning light. She was thankful her niece wasn't within earshot. After breakfast, Carter had donned an old pair of sweats and was safely in the back yard, helping Uncle Miltie stir compost. "Once something happens, it may be too late. Isn't there anything you can do, Herb? *Anything?*"

"You don't even know if the guy with the old yellow Norton has anything to do with it."

"He's watching her, Herb. We've all seen him."

Willow Bend's chief of police took a deep breath. "Okay.

I'll have one of my guys keep a look-out. Drive by the house. And I'll put out a local bulletin on the bike. Maybe they'll get a chance to find out who this guy is. But that's all I can do right now."

"Well, I'm grateful for that. Thank you, Herb." Gracie now had Part A of her plan to protect her niece set in motion, but she still had to figure out Part B: how to make sure Carter Stephens was never left alone. That wasn't a problem around the house or even in town. What had hampered her sleep was the vision of Carter, running or biking alone along a deserted rural road. She needed a training buddy, beginning *now*.

Gracie didn't have to think twice.

"Hello?"

"Don," she said, "it's Gracie."

"Hey, there! Thanks again for a great party."

"You're welcome." She then went straight to the point. "I need to ask a favor."

"Anything for you, Gracie. You know that."

"Thanks." She hesitated, worried about getting the words right. Last night, Carter had begged her relatives not to tell anyone other than the police about the secret admirer. Reluctantly, Gracie and Uncle Miltie had agreed. "I'm not sure if Carter mentioned this to you, but she's training for a charity marathon."

"Uh huh. She said she was really enjoying the workouts."

"She is, but . . . ."

"But . . . what?"

"Well, she needs to run or bike for long distances and . . ." here she crossed her fingers, hoping God would forgive her a small white lie. "She was asking Uncle Miltie and me for route ideas. Seems she doesn't like to retrace her steps and needs a variety of terrain to help build up her muscles. Well, neither of us would know where to start. Then, I thought of you! You exercise regularly. I was wondering if you'd train with her? Show her some local byways." She added the finishing touch. "I *know* she'd enjoy your company."

"Well, I'm not so sure about that."

"What do you mean?"

"She didn't even . . . oh, uh . . . never mind. Of course, I could take her out. Has she already worked out today?"

"No. She's battling compost with Uncle Miltie at the moment, but she mentioned something about a seven-mile run later."

"I know the perfect route," he assured her. "Why don't you have her call me when she comes in?"

"Great, Don. That's what I was hoping you'd say. Thanks."

She hung up, now one happy guardian angel. Part B was off the drawing board.

The phone rang.

She grabbed the receiver and immediately asked, "You haven't changed your mind, have you?"

"What?" a muffled voice replied. "Mrs. Parks? Is that you?"

"I'm sorry." Gracie thought she recognized the voice. "Becky? Are you all right, dear?"

"No, Mrs. Parks," Rebecca Baxter wailed. "Everything's falling apart!" She blew her nose. "Do you think . . . *please,* could you meet me? I really need your help."

"Now?"

"If you could," the young woman replied, sobbing. "I'm in the park on the bench near the kids' swings."

What on earth could be wrong? "I know the spot, dear. I'll be there in a few minutes. Just hang on, okay?"

Gracie headed to the back yard. Immediately her spirits lifted as she saw her relatives, shoulder to shoulder, shoveling grass clippings onto the compost heap.

"Carter, dear? May I speak with you a moment?"

"Sure, Aunt Gracie," the young woman replied, setting down her spade. Breathing heavily, Uncle Miltie grabbed the chance to lean on the handle of his. "Everything all right?"

"Perfectly. I've got a little errand to run, but I was just speaking with Don."

Carter smiled.

"He'd like to go for a run with you this afternoon and asked that you give him a call."

"Does he?" Carter replied, running a gloved hand across her brow. "What a sweet man! Sure. It'd be nice to have some company. Thanks, Aunt Gracie. I'll phone him in a few minutes."

"Better wash your face before you go," Uncle Miltie instructed, pointing to the dirt on Carter's gloves.

She laughed. "It's a run, Uncle Miltie. Not a date."

17

HEAD IN HANDS, Becky Baxter sat dejectedly on a park bench directly across from the children's sand box. Nearby, a pair of red-headed kids swung from the monkey bars and a trio of toddlers explored the play structure while their mothers watched and chatted. Gracie steered Fannie Mae into a parking spot, then walked over to join her young friend.

Becky heard her approach and turned. Gracie's heart lurched to see the scarlet blotches of anguish discoloring her face. Immediately, she took both of the girl's hands in hers and gripped gently.

"It's going to be all right, dear," she said automatically, pushing aside an envelope to join her on the bench. "Just take a deep breath and tell me what happened."

High peals of children's laughter floated in their direction.

Becky took a long breath, then released a torrent of words, none of which Gracie understood.

"Whoa!" she finally interrupted, offering a fresh tissue. "That's way too fast, Becky. Please, try again. Slowly now. Okay?"

Her companion dabbed at her brimming eyes and gulped. "Evvverything's all wrooong, Mrs. Parks," she began shakily. Gracie's gaze never wavered. Rebecca paused, collecting herself. When she spoke again, her voice was calm. "I'm living a lie, Mrs. Parks. A lie!"

Gracie hesitated, not sure what to say.

It didn't matter. The floodgates had opened and all she had to do was stand firm and let the torrent spill over her.

"I *hate* finance. It's cold, *ruthless*. I tried. I really did, but it's all about profits, money markets and inflation rates." She paused for a breath. "Soulless." She shuddered. "And I can't *bear* the thought of working in a bank or a law office. Oh, dear heaven, Mrs. Parks, I'd rather die! I . . . I can't, *I won't*, think that way. Carter's got the right idea. I'm sure she could get a lot more money somewhere else, but she stays in the DA's office because she's sticking to her principles and doing what she loves. That's really wonderful. Oh, there's so much more I want to do, to give, than burn out working for some big corporation. Why can't I be brave like Carter?"

She closed her eyes and finished in a whisper. "It . . . it's just not right." Her eyes suddenly popped open, startling Gracie. "God doesn't want me to be miserable, does He?"

"Of course not, dear," Gracie replied soothingly. "He

wants you to be happy, to use your gifts in His honor." She leaned toward Rebecca. "But, you already know that, dear. In your heart. What's stopping you?"

As quickly as it had burst, the dam dried up and Rebecca bit her lower lip and fell silent.

Gracie waited, the silence punctuated only by the nearby screech of a reluctant metal swing.

"My father," Becky finally whispered. She looked at Gracie. "He wants so much for me! I . . . I know he wants me to be happy but . . . he thinks I can find it in *his* work. He's a good banker, Mrs. Parks. Honest, hard-working, more compassionate than most, yet, I know it's a job he settled for, not a career he loves. At least, in the beginning, he did it because he had to take care of us. Now, I don't think he knows anymore. It's become who he is." A slight smile lifted her lips. "Willow Bend's most popular mortgage broker. I know that's what folks call him."

"Is that so bad?"

"No. Of course not. It's just . . . it's just not me."

"Have you told him how you feel?"

Becky prodded a bit of pink gum marring the bench's armrest. "Not lately. We got into too many fights in the past, and they upset all of us, so I wound up giving in. I didn't want to disappoint him, Mrs. Parks. Or my mom. I know what they've done for me, the sacrifices they've made and I'm grateful."

She rubbed furiously.

"I thought I could hang in there, swallow my desires and just do it. But it's making me *miserable*. It wouldn't even be so bad if dad would at least accept Dennis. It was tough enough secretly dating him when we were both in college but now, with Dennis following his own crazy star, my father thinks even less of him. Keeps reminding me that he's the poor guy who's had to foreclose many family farms. But what Dennis is doing is crazy only if you can't see his vision."

She shook her head. "What my father doesn't realize is that marrying Dennis and building the new vegetable business with him, that's *exactly* the life I want. Not apartment living in a big city, working every minute for someone else. I don't care how much money I could make!" Becky paused, and a large tear trickled down her cheek. "But now, Dennis is backing away. Says he doesn't want to cause a permanent rift between me and my family, and . . . I'm worried. Maybe's he really losing interest. He's such a great guy."

She clasped her hands together. "Maybe he's even found someone else and doesn't want to tell me." But she looked doubtful

"You still love him?"

Becky smiled proudly. "Never stopped." She took a breath, then went on. "Another little lie. We just pretended to break up when we went to college, to make my parents happy. Oh! I almost forgot. I owe you an apology. In town the other day, I deliberately avoided you. I'm really sorry, but I didn't want you to tell my dad that you'd seen me with Dennis. Isn't that childish?"

"That's all right, dear." Gracie shifted position and felt something poking her leg. "What's this?"

"Oh, something I wanted to show you." Becky picked up the envelope, reached inside and shyly handed Gracie a sheaf of papers. "It's nothing really. Just a story. At least, that's what my dad thinks."

"And you?"

Becky bit her lip. "Well, it's more than that. At least, I think so. It's what I love to do. What I want to do. What God put me on earth to do. But my dad, he's a numbers guy . . . he just can't see writing as anything but a hobby." She lowered her voice, imitating her father. "Do you know how many starving writers there are in this country, young lady? Well, I do. Thousands. Almost as many as there are foreclosed farms."

She squeezed her eyes shut, as though blocking out his discouraging words. "Can you help me, Mrs. Parks? Would you read it, let me know what you think? My dad respects you. If you liked it, maybe . . . maybe you could talk to him for me?"

Gracie started to refuse, to say that she was the wrong person to ask, to explain that she had no literary expertise with which to judge, but she was too touched to do anything other than accept Becky's trust. "Of course, I'll read it," she replied, taking the papers. "I'd be honored. And I'll do whatever I can to help."

The young woman now threw her arms around Gracie. Then she pulled back, wiped her eyes and said, "I'd better be going. My mom's taking me to lunch. I don't know how to thank you, Mrs. Parks."

Gracie smiled. "No need. Give your mother my regards." She started praying as the young woman waved and strolled out of the park. *I'm counting on You, dear Lord. I'm sure You put me in this situation to help this poor child out. I just wish You would let me know what I'm supposed to do.*

She felt the paper in her hand and glanced down. The title of Becky's short story was "Embracing the Road Less Traveled," and Gracie was heartened by its reference to the Robert Frost poem. One of her favorites. She had always loved it, especially the last line, with its "promises to keep."

Gracie began to read Becky's narrative journey, recalling the first few months of Dennis McIver's progress in growing new lettuces and vegetables for the gourmet market.

After the first few lines, she found herself under the young woman's spell. Becky's ability to bring to life this contemporary tale of a farmer's quest for survival was truly heartwarming. Through the simple but powerful language, Gracie practically tasted the spring winds and felt the seeds' rough texture.

And she laughed out loud when Becky described her own mangled attempts at pronouncing *mizuna, radicchio,* and *arugula,* while helping to market Dennis's lettuce. Gracie, too, shared the disheartening effects of the lack of family support. Becky, she thought, had a true gift for filtering life through language!

The brief essay evoked a proud agricultural past while tenderly questioning the viability of modern family farms. It boldly welcomed innovative agricultural practices. The message was both pragmatic and promising.

Well, Lord, this young woman truly honors You. Her words, Your words, need to be read by people far and wide. We've abandoned our roots and forgotten our relationship to the land. We need to understand both the joys and sorrows of rural life, to recognize its values, and to act with compassion and support those brave souls who crave its bittersweet harvests. Rebecca Baxter and Dennis McIver, and others like them, deserve our support. Thanks to You, Lord, that is something I can now provide.

"THERE'S SUN-SHINE in my soul to-day, More glor-i-ous and bright. Than glows in an-y earth-ly skies, For Je-sus is my light." Though Gracie had started singing softly while praise-walking into town, she couldn't contain herself. The key of A flat was one of her favorites and so she let loose on a deserted stretch with the refrain: "O there's sun—shine, bles-sed sun—shine, When the peace-ful hap-py moments roll; When Je-sus shows His smil-ing face, There is sun-shine in the soul."

And indeed there was! The leafy streets of Willow Bend were bathed in a dappled golden hue. Brilliant early-morning light bounced off windows and pavement, sparkling rainbow-like as she strode by gardens thick with flowers. There was nothing quite so satisfying as pushing oneself physically while singing God's praises. Her mind, spirit and body were one, tuned to His word, ready for His command. As she marched downtown, Gracie Parks reveled in the glorious infusion of hope and vitality. She so loved the Lord and cherished His blessings!

As she slowed down, Gracie mentally checked off this day's major godsends: Carter was safe, hiking with Don this morning; her uncle's osteoarthritis was improving with the heat; and, finally, God had graced her with a couple of ideas that might help Rebecca and Dennis.

Breezing down Main Street, she checked her watch against the stained glass clock on the corner, before arriving at the entrance to the *Mason County Gazette*. Rocky was standing in his office, his phone against his ear. He caught her eye and waved her in. She settled in the big chair opposite his cluttered desk.

"Look, Mike," Rocky was saying. "No excuses. We need that story nailed down by this afternoon. Yeah, I know politicians march to their own drummer, but we've got a deadline." He listened for a few seconds, pacing behind the desk. "Okay, okay. It's yours. Just have it logged in the computer by three."

"Problem?" Gracie asked, as he replaced the receiver.

Rocky rewarded her with a mischievous grin. "Are you kidding?"

Gracie was momentarily confused. "But, you sounded . . . like something was wrong."

The editor ran his fingers through his salt-and-pepper hair. "The day you come into my office, my dear lady, and I'm not pressing my staff on some story, that's the day I hang up my press pass. Even here in Willow Bend, the news waits for no one!"

She smiled.

"So, you were going to buy me a coffee?"

"If you have the time."

"For you. Always."

He dug into a drawer and stuffed something into his pocket before marching around his desk and shouting to Sue Jameson that he'd be gone for half an hour.

On the way to Abe's, they chatted about the croquet tournament. "You know," Rocky said, opening the deli's front door. A hint of cinnamon greeted them. Several booths were already occupied, as well as half of the red-padded stools. "I got all the way home before I realized I had mixed up the Turner twins."

Gracie called a hello to busy Abe. He smiled and waved them to an open booth. "No wonder Lester kept poking me every couple of minutes," Rocky finished.

"You're not the first one," she laughed. "And you won't be the last."

"Do you think I've offended them?" he asked, sliding in across from her and laying his cell phone to one side.

Gracie shook her head. "Not in the least, my friend. I think they'll have been flattered. Why else would they dress alike at their age?"

"Good point."

"Coffee, folks?" Abe asked, pot in one hand, two mugs in the other.

"Fill 'em up," Rocky replied, sniffing slightly. "Say, do I smell cinnamon twists?"

Abe grinned. "Trust a newshound to have the best nose in town. They came out of the oven not fifteen minutes ago."

Rocky raised a bushy eyebrow at Gracie, something that always made her smile. She had even tried it a few times, in front of the mirror, but couldn't get the knack. "Come on, old girl. You *walked* here, didn't you? You actually *owe* yourself one, in my opinion."

"Well . . ."

"Then that'll be two," Rocky instructed. "On me."

"I thought you told Sue you'd be back in half an hour."

"What's the point of being the owner if you can't play hooky now and again?"

He then said to her, "That was another great party. Not everyone has the knack for ensuring that everyone enjoys themselves the way you do."

"Don't forget, I had lots of loving support from Uncle Miltie, as usual, and from Carter, too. That can make all the difference."

"Maybe. But it's still the person with the byline who tells

the story. By the way, how's she doing? Hasn't she lost some weight?"

Gracie didn't want to lie but couldn't break her promise. "She's fine," she answered. "A little thinner, yes, but she's training for a marathon. In fact, she's out with Don now, running for several miles."

"Oh, so that's how the wind blows? It's always been obvious that he's a charter member of the Carter Stephens fan club!"

Gracie agreed. "That's true, but I'm not sure what Carter thinks. She's almost too busy to have someone in her life at the moment."

"I'm not surprised. Her job's a demanding one."

"Sometimes I worry she'll wait too long. I'm all for having a career, but I also know how important it is to love someone and share your life. I don't want her to miss that."

Rocky toyed with his coffee mug. "It's tough these days for women, isn't it? They want the challenge and gratification of work, and I, for one, believe they deserve it. But at the same time, they're still the ones giving birth and taking most of the responsibility for the children, aren't they?"

Gracie gazed with fresh respect at her friend.

He flushed. "A lot of women work in the news business. I've had my share of star reporters torn between getting the scoop and picking up the kids. It's not easy." He sighed and reached into his pocket for his wallet. "For editors, either."

"What are they?" Gracie asked, staring at the brightly colored triangles of cloth that slipped out along with Rocky's billfold.

Rocky grinned and passed them over to Gracie. "Bandannas. Red one's for Rover and the blue's for Gent. For the Blessing Service. What do you think?"

"I don't know. I thought Gent was a yellow sort of guy! But I'll trust your fashion sense!"

They both laughed.

"How's the organizing going? People are bad enough, but it must be something else to plan for animals."

"We're pretty well on track," Gracie replied. "I'm not worried about logistics or even dog fights but . . ."

"But what?"

"I've had some doubts about the legitimacy of giving such special treatment to creatures when there are so many needy human beings all around us."

Rocky considered this. "But they're *God's* creatures, aren't they?"

She nodded.

"Well, given the friendship and love they freely give us, it seems to me that they deserve some kindness and respect in return. Where better than in God's own house? You haven't restricted attendance to folks with pets, have you?"

"Of course not. Eternal Hope is always open to everyone."

"Well, there you go. Everyone's welcome and anyone who attends is going to benefit, right?"

"Right," Gracie replied. Who'd ever have thought he'd so perfectly grasp the principle? "Thank you, Rocky."

"Not needed. I may not be religious, but I'm looking forward to being there. No one else would ever have had the idea, Gracie, much less the ability to pull it off. *Thank you.*"

Gracie thought now was the perfect time to make her request. "Well, since you're feeling so beholden, may I ask a favor?"

"Any time."

She reached into her little knapsack and pulled out an envelope. "Would you read this and tell me your honest opinion?"

He raised an eyebrow. "Are you after my job, now?"

Gracie smiled. "No. Becky Baxter, Fred's daughter, wrote it. Personally, I think it deserves to be published, but your professional opinion would be a big help."

His cell phone began to play "The Star-Spangled Banner." "Consider it done," he replied, reaching forward. Just before he punched the on button, he hesitated. "You know I'm going to give you the truth, no sugar coating?"

She nodded and pointed to their empty plates. "I've had all the sugar I need."

19

IT'S SO KIND OF YOU to do this, Mrs. Parks," Becky Baxter said, as Fannie Mae rolled along the streets of Willow Bend.

Upon her return from Abe's, Gracie had managed to do a load of washing and pay a few bills before noon. Grabbing an apple to munch, she'd made her uncle a cold ham sandwich before heading out after one to pick up her young friend.

"I know I've met the Searfosses," Becky continued, "at church functions, but we've never really spoken. My mom mentioned Anna in her letters to me at college, after her books were reprinted. I never realized until then that we had a literary celebrity in our congregation."

Gracie flipped the signal to indicate a left-hand turn. "You're going to love Anna and Joe. They're fine people, very kind and generous. We've been friends for years." She brought the car to a stop in front of a tidy little bungalow.

"I'm not sure if your mom told you but Anna's losing her sight, poor dear. Complications of diabetes."

Becky nodded. "A terrible blow for a writer. Not being able to read."

"You'd never know it from her attitude. She's an inspiration, in more ways than one." Gracie smiled and patted her companion's hand. "That's why I want you to meet her."

Joe had the door open before they were even halfway up the walk. "Gracie! So good to see you." The elderly man turned and shouted inside. "Anna, Gracie's here!"

Gracie hugged him as she reached the stoop, then introduced Rebecca.

"Fred's daughter, right?" he said, vigorously shaking her hand. "You've changed! All grown up."

Becky laughed.

"Come in, come in! My wife's dying to meet you."

Joe led them into a cozy living room. Anna Searfoss sat on the couch facing the doorway.

Gracie went to give her friend a hug. "It's good to see you," she said. "I'm sorry I didn't get a chance to chat last Sunday."

Anna smiled, clasping Gracie's hands. "That's all right. I know you're busy with the preparations for the Blessing Service."

"Well, I shouldn't be too busy for you and Joe! But here's someone I've been promising a chance to meet you!" She quickly introduced Becky. Anna patted the seat beside her, encouraging the young woman to sit.

"Gracie tells me you're a writer," Anna said.

The young woman nodded.

Gracie mouthed the words, "Out loud."

Becky spoke up cheerfully, "Yes. I *love* to write. I have all my life, ever since I was little."

Anna smiled. "My mother used to say I'd rather scribble than eat."

Her husband, who like Gracie sat in one of the matching wing chairs, laughed. "Speaking of which, how about a cup of tea and some of my Anna's lemon-cherry loaf?"

The guests murmured their pleasure. Joe beamed.

"Tell me about yourself, dear," Anna suggested.

"I'll give you a hand," Gracie said, following Joe into the blue-and-white tiled kitchen. Behind her, she could hear Anna and Rebecca already deep in discussion.

He grinned as he filled the kettle. "This is so nice of you, Gracie. Ever since she left the library, Anna's been short of kindred spirits. And with her failing eyesight...it's not easy. Literature was her daily pleasure." He got out a flowered plate. "I'm not much good in that respect. I never understood how she put two words together, much less a whole series of children's books."

Gracie told him, "It's a blessing. And that's why, when

Becky showed me her story, I immediately thought of her. Anna's the only one I know who can really understand what Becky wants to do." She laid dishes and tea cups on a sturdy tray. "Poor child, she really needs the empathy a listener like Anna can provide. She's not getting much support."

"I guess it's to be expected. In many ways, Fred's a lot like me, except he delivers money where I delivered furniture." Joe shrugged and led the way back into the living room. "Neither of us are what you'd call artistic."

Becky was holding one of Anna's newly reprinted books. She turned to Gracie, her face awestruck. "Look at this, Mrs. Parks!" She reverently held up a book titled *The Butterfly Festival at Lazy Lake*, pointing to a stack at her elbow. "And there are nine more!"

Gracie set down the tray. "They're wonderful, I know."

Becky leaned back, clasping the book to her chest. "What's wonderful is having someone in Willow Bend like Anna!"

Her hostess' ailing eyes sparkled with tears of pleasure. She then asked, "Tell me about *your* writing, dear."

Becky paused. "Well, I'm not really sure how to describe it, Mrs. Searfoss." She hesitated another moment. "I . . . like to write about what's going on in my life. Not exactly a journal, you understand, more like crafting a story around something I know personally."

"Purely autobiographical or fictionalized versions?"

The young woman smiled. "A little of both. I guess what I do is take a real-life incident and massage it, expanding it beyond reality to make a point."

It was Anna's turn to smile. "Would you read us something of yours?"

Becky looked apprehensive. Then, letting out a breath, she asked shyly, "Are you sure you all want to listen?"

"Of course," Joe replied. "Been looking forward to it since Gracie's call, haven't we?"

"Well, I've never read out loud to anyone before."

"It'll be good practice," Anna said, "for your book signings."

Becky shot her a grateful look. Then, realizing that Anna couldn't see, she emphasized how much that meant to her, even if her hostess was only being polite. "Okay, here goes," she added, inhaling deeply. "This one's called, 'Raising the Roof.'"

At first, her voice was tentative. Then, slowly she gained confidence from the nods and smiles of her tiny audience. All three listeners seemed enthralled at the vivid picture painted by her words. The poignant yet amusing story of a young couple's struggle to rebuild an old barn generated tears and laughter. It was a wholesome story, filled with faith, and demonstrating that in any era—even one obsessed with technology—what was truly essential to survival was family, neighbors and the love of God.

When she was finished, they were silent. Finally, Anna reached over to take Becky's hands. "That's beautiful, dear. Absolutely beautiful. Wasn't it, Joe?"

"First rate!" Joe crowed.

"It's lovely, my dear," Gracie added. "Truly lovely. Anna's quite right."

"I didn't think too many young people cared about life's simple pleasures anymore, what with jetting around from continent to continent and thinking the gospel comes from the Internet," the elderly woman said. "But to think that another young Willow Bend woman is following in my footsteps, writing from the heart about faith, family and love of the land," Anna said, clasping her hands, "Why, it's almost a miracle, isn't it, Joe?"

"It surely is," he replied, his lined face shining. "It surely is."

"So, you've been spending a lot of time on Dennis's farm?" Gracie asked as she drove Becky home.

"Every time I come home, which isn't really very much." She hung her head. "I tell my parents I'm visiting girlfriends or going to the library. It's wrong, I know but . . ."

"Attempting to farm in new ways takes a lot of courage," Gracie said, slowing to let two boys rollerblade across the road. "I know Dennis' family isn't too . . ." she paused, slightly embarrassed to be hinting at the McIvers's disharmony, then quickly continued, "What I mean is, Don Delano mentioned that he's helped out a bit and that Dennis apparently could use more than a couple of pairs of hands."

"Like right now," Becky said. "He's picking every day. Fortunately, he's got a guy helping out, but I'll go by later on."

"Oh?"

"Uh huh. Kind of a funny coincidence. The guy's bike had broken down, about a mile down the road from Dennis's farm. Dennis is real handy with motors, so the guy offered to help out with the harvest if Dennis would fix his bike. Now, he's crashing in the barn, staying for a while."

Gracie barely heard the last sentence, her mind was still replaying the word *motors*. "What sort of motorcycle was it?" she asked, her voice deliberately casual.

Becky looked at her.

Gracie shrugged sheepishly. "Uncle Miltie will ask."

The girl frowned. "Don't know. It's big, real old, and a funny color."

"Oh?" Gracie said, her fingers squeezing the steering wheel.

"Yeah. For a guy's bike, that is. It's yellow."

Gracie had to laugh at Becky's reaction to what she said next. "Gotcha!" she exclaimed.

"Got whom, Mrs. Parks?" her passenger inquired innocently.

20

AS GRACIE PULLED into her driveway, she noticed Don Delano's car parked out front. Dressed in a sweat-soaked blue T-shirt and baggy shorts, he was pouring orange juice as Gracie entered through the kitchen door. Uncle Miltie and Carter—a towel wrapped around her shoulders—were seated, already with glasses in their hands. Gooseberry dropped from a kitchen chair and trotted over to her. With a huge yawn, he collapsed on his side and wriggled, offering her his tummy.

"Hey, Gracie," Don said. "Want something to drink?"

"No, thanks." She ruffled her cat's soft fur, then gave her uncle and niece a quick hug. "How did it go?" she asked, settling into a chair. In a flash, she had a kneading, purring lump in her lap.

Don drained his glass. "She pretty nearly wore me out, Gracie," he confessed.

Carter laughed. "Ha! I had to push myself to keep up. I think I may have convinced him to try the marathon, though."

Uncle Miltie pulled the cookie jar within striking distance. "Don't know what's gotten into you young folks these days. You seem to do everything—work or play—at breakneck speed. It's almost as if you're rushing through life, trying to get ahead. I'm afraid that you don't appreciate that it's the journey that really counts." He looked down at his own weak legs. "Anyway, twenty-six miles of pounding the pavement. That can't be good for anyone's body, young or old."

"Actually," Carter said, "I've never felt better. If you're looking to burn calories, build bones, reduce stress and increase your cardio-vascular capabilities, it's hard to find a workout that costs less and takes less time. After a run, I feel relaxed, empowered, focused. In fact, it's amazing how in touch with yourself you become when you're working out. Don't you find, Don?"

Don nodded. "Not only that, it's great thinking time. I get most of my lesson plans worked through during a run."

"Exactly! I used to have trouble finding enough concentrated time during the day to plan case strategies. Now, when I'm on the move, it's as though my brain's set free. I'm able to work the whole scenario through, imagining the defense's rebuttals and counter strategies. I bet I'm ten times more efficient thinking during a run than in our busy office."

"How do you remember everything?" Gracie asked. "Do you stop and jot it down?"

Carter reached into her fanny pack and tugged free a small black rectangle. "This does the trick," she replied, turning on the tiny tape recorder for demonstration.

"Maybe you're more efficient," Uncle Miltie conceded reluctantly. "But I wonder. Life goes by at a pretty fair clip whether we're running or standing still. A few more miles under your belts, you'll soon see." He bit into a cookie, then said, "All this talk about exercise reminds me of the guy who lost his pants while running." He paused, cookie suspended in his hand.

Carter moaned. Don studiously cleaned his glasses.

Uncle Miltie grinned. "Come on, Gracie: ask if they were loose."

Gracie looked up from tickling Gooseberry's chin. "I'll bite. Were they loose?"

Her uncle slapped his thigh. "No, but the neighbor's dog was."

"Ha, ha," said Carter. "Very funny."

Don rose. "Well, I guess I'd better go. Really enjoyed getting out there with you, Carter."

The young woman stood. "Me, too. It's nice to have company."

Don smiled. "How about a movie, sometime?"

Carter hesitated.

"Uh," Don said, swallowing hard. "I meant with a group." He edged to the doorway. "You know, Les, Rick and Comfort, too, if they can get a sitter. No big deal."

Carter rubbed her face with the towel. "I'm not sure about my schedule. Let me get back to you, okay?"

Gracie gently pulled her reluctant cat off her lap and placed him on the floor. "Wait, Don. I'll walk you out."

Don didn't say anything until they reached his car. "Is everything all right with Carter?" he asked finally. "I didn't mean to put any pressure on her."

Gracie shook her head. "It's not you, believe me."

"What's going on?"

Biting her lower lip, Gracie replied, "I'm sorry. She's . . . she's just a bit preoccupied, that's all."

Don yanked open the driver's door. "I'll say! One minute, she's chatting away happily, the next, it's like she's gone to the moon." He started the engine. "Guess I blew it with the flowers."

Gracie blinked. "Flowers? What flowers?"

For a moment, the sun reflected off Don's wire-rims, shielding his eyes. "Yellow roses."

"*You* sent them?"

He nodded, putting the vehicle in gear.

"Why didn't you say something?"

Don looked straight ahead. "Nobody mentioned them

when I arrived. So, I thought they hadn't come. But then . . . then I saw them in the garbage." He paused glumly. "That said it all."

Before she could reply, he drove away.

"*Don* sent the flowers?" Carter asked.

Gracie nodded.

Uncle Miltie frowned. "Why didn't he say something?"

"It was a mix-up, from the very beginning," Gracie replied. "Cart—uh, we all jumped to the conclusion that they were sent by the stalker. Don happened to see them in the garbage and jumped to his own misguided conclusion."

"Poor Don," Carter exclaimed. "I feel terrible! I'm going to give him a call and apologize, right now." While she dialed, Gracie asked her uncle if he had the envelope that arrived with the chocolates. She wanted to examine the handwriting.

The elderly man thought for a second. "That rings a bell. I'll go check the laundry. I remember holding on to one of those cards."

Carter hung up the phone. "No answer."

Uncle Miltie returned slowly a couple of minutes later, shaking his head. "Sorry, but I can't find it."

"Find what?" Carter asked.

"The envelope that came with the chocolates. I thought Uncle Miltie put it in his pocket but now . . ."

He leaned against the table to spread out his hands in disgust. "Danged if I know what happened to it. I must have dropped it somewhere. It's got to be somewhere, but, anyway, it may not have been the one that came with the candy."

Carter gave him a quick squeeze. "Not to worry. Unfortunately, I'm still pretty sure I know who sent *them*."

21

THE NEXT MORNING, Gracie was in the church office, finishing up some filing for Pat Allen. She and Marge often volunteered to help out, knowing how papers piled up there.

"Well, that's it for this month," she told the church secretary.

Pat looked suitably grateful. "Thanks, Gracie. It was awfully kind of you to take Marge's turn."

"I enjoy it. There's something very satisfying about making order out of chaos. Everything in its place." She paused, reminded of the confusion of the last few days. "Too bad we can't do the same with our lives."

Pat raised her eyebrows. "Everything all right?"

"Of course. Nothing serious, just the usual mix-ups and misunderstandings."

"Well, one may have crosses to bear," Pat began, "but they can also be ladders that lead to heaven."

Gracie smiled. "One hopes so! Anyway, everything all set for the service?"

"Almost. Still having trouble finding someone to help with building the platform. I'd kind of hoped that Don would offer, seeing how he's off in the summer—but he seems to be busy."

Gracie felt a trifle guilty. Because of her, Don was spending much of his free time with Carter. Gracie disliked inconveniencing her church or its activities in any way, but neither was she willing to increase Carter's vulnerability. There had to be another way. "We've still got a few days. I'm sure we'll find someone," she said, trying to sound more confident than she felt.

"You really want to serve *salads* after the blessing of the animals?" Dennis McIver asked.

"Yes. We're going to be outdoors and need something simple," Gracie replied, adjusting the telephone against her chin. "I thought it would be nice to try your some of your new lettuces and other produce. That is, if you can spare it."

"Spare it! Of course I can," he replied, his voice rising in enthusiasm. "I think it's a swell idea, Mrs. Parks! Once you've tasted mine, you'll never go back to stuff like that iceberg junk."

Gracie murmured agreement.

"You know, Mrs. Parks? I was thinking of not coming.

I'm not that popular with my family at the moment. It was probably going to be simpler for me to skip it. But, I've got to tell you, I sure wish everyone your age had your attitude." He paused. "If I could just get my granddad to even taste my stuff, man, that would be something. He can be such a stubborn grouch sometimes! I'm surprised you're even calling, come to think about it. I'm sure he's told you that I've flipped out."

"He hasn't told me anything," she replied honestly, choosing not to mention his grandmother's concerns. "I know Ben can be a bit difficult sometimes, but you know what I've found? No matter how crusty a person is, there's always a cream filling inside."

Dennis gave a hoot of laughter. "How'd you find out about the produce, anyway?"

"For one thing, this is Willow Bend, remember? But, also, both Becky and Don have been raving about your farming success. She's a lovely young woman, Dennis. You're a lucky fellow."

There was a long pause. "She told you about us?"

"She thinks the world of you and wants to build a life with you. Do you know that?"

Silence.

"Dennis, you'll forgive me if I say that response doesn't breed confidence."

"Don't get me wrong, Mrs. Parks. I'm crazy about Becky and want to marry her but . . ."

"But what?"

"I'm not sure being a farmer's wife is the best thing for *her*. She's real smart, you know. Top of her class in college. I know her parents, they want more for her. Especially her dad." He hesitated for a long time. Gracie was just about to say something when Dennis continued softly, "Why do parents expect their children to live out their dreams?"

"Do they?"

"Well, ours sure do. Becky's dad is set on her being some big-shot financier—he keeps coming out to my farm to lecture me—and my folks want me to farm just the way they do. They're so busy planning our lives, they don't even listen to us."

Gracie didn't know what to say. It was so often the truth. She remembered how hard it was for Elmo and her to let go and allow Arlen to make his own way in the world. And when that path led away from Willow Bend, all the way to New York City, it had almost broken their hearts.

"I'm not sure how your mom and dad think but I can understand their fears. As a parent, you just want what you think is best for your child, but I know from experience that that's not necessarily what *is* best. When our son left home, left Willow Bend, we had a difficult time understanding. We prayed for help and found it in our very own pastor. He said we should be proud of our son's initiative and ambition and quoted a little phrase to us. He thought it suited. I'll never forget it."

"What was it?"

"'Do not follow where the path may lead. Go instead where there is no path and leave a trail.'"

Dennis was silent, then gave a soft whistle. "Wow. That hits the nail square on the head."

"Perhaps your parents need a little more time," she added, recognizing the platitude even as she said it. "Who knows? It's possible they'll be won over at the service. Oh, and by the way, Becky mentioned someone—a stranger—who's been helping you out. Please let him know that he'd be most welcome."

She was relieved to hear Dennis chuckle. "I will, Mrs. Parks, but I wouldn't hold my breath. He's pretty anti-social."

"A fever of one-hundred and three?" Gracie sank unhappily into her kitchen chair, picturing her little grandson lying wanly in his bed. "My poor Elmo. Oh, Arlen, honey, that's serious! Have you taken him to a doctor?"

"Of course, mom. Now, take it easy, okay? I didn't call you to set you off worrying. Our pediatrician assures us that little

El's going to be fine. It's just the flu. Half the kids in his day camp are down with it."

"May I say hello to him?"

"Sorry, mom. He's asleep. We'll call back in a day or so, when he's feeling better." Her son sighed. "I'm real sorry we're not going to make the Blessing Service. We were all looking forward to getting out of the city, but the doctor thinks it might be too much too soon. How's everything shaping up?"

"Fine, really, though of course I'm disappointed that you aren't coming. By the way," she added, brightening her voice, "Carter's here for a visit."

"Is she? Hey, that's great!"

"She's in training, for a marathon."

"Good for her! Last time we spoke, it was all work, no play. Tell her I'm glad she's taking some time for herself."

Gracie assured her only son that she would. "How are things at the dance studio? I guess with summer almost over, Wendy's fall classes must be filling up?"

"Folks are just trickling in now, but we expect a flood in the next couple of weeks. Seems everybody gets out of New York in early August. Oh, you'll never guess who I ran into!"

"Who?"

"Spike O'Neal, though now he goes by his real name of Arthur."

"Spike?" A picture of a teenager with frizzy, dishwater-colored hair and extensive acne floated into her mind. "The boy with the wild hair and skin problems?"

Arlen laughed. "That's him. Or at least, that's what he was like in high school. You wouldn't recognize him now! Very slick! An orthodontist, can you believe that? I've never seen whiter, straighter teeth."

Gracie was preoccupied, her thoughts drifting into the past, to Arlen's high school graduation. Her son had been so handsome in his black gown and tasseled mortar board.

Arlen was still speaking. ". . . came to Wendy's studio last Saturday to enroll his daughter."

But Gracie was only half listening. She had walked into the living room, and was peering at the wall of photographs facing her, her eyes falling immediately on the graduation photograph. She recognized the two young men grinning alongside her son. Spike O'Neal and Jeff . . . Jeff Mcsomething. "Isn't Spike one of the boys who—"

"Yeah, mom." For a split second, Arlen sounded like a little boy caught in the act. "Gosh, you have a memory like an elephant!"

Gracie reached out to touch the tiny face of her son, peering out from within the frame. "Well, dear, you have to admit that was one of your least endearing pranks."

"I know, I know. But," her son replied. "*Please, please,*

promise me you'll never, ever tell Elmo! He imagines I was perfect as a kid. I want to keep up that misunderstanding as long as possible."

"Oh, don't worry, dear. You were perfect," Gracie replied, savoring the tide of memories. "A *perfectly* normal boy."

OVER THE NEXT COUPLE OF DAYS, Gracie's household continued its pleasant routine. In the mornings, Gracie and Gooseberry rose early to praise-walk and Carter disappeared to train with Don. After a leisurely breakfast, Gracie and her uncle tidied up the garden, beating the afternoon heat. In the early afternoon, Uncle Miltie snoozed on the front porch and Carter headed into the dining room to catch up on her work. Gracie, meanwhile, puttered about, happily completing small domestic tasks, such as turning up her new jeans and relining her dresser drawers.

Just before seven-thirty on Thursday morning, she was striding hard, practicing "All Things Bright and Beautiful" and approaching the end of her walk. She especially liked the last verse, and as Gooseberry sidled along a picket fence across the street, Gracie bellowed out, *"He gave us eyes to see them, and lips that we might tell how great is God Almighty who has made all things well."*

Her cat seemed to appreciate the sentiment for when she finished, he stopped, spun and sprawled on the sidewalk. Gracie grinned and pushed her tired legs another thirty feet to join him. Holding the fence for balance, she gently stretched her back and neck muscles. Inhaling the scent of climbing roses, she let her mind wander over upcoming duties. The arrangements for the Blessing Service were complete, except for the building of the platform.

For some reason, instead of being pricked by concern, she felt unusually calm, certain that someone would "turnip," as her uncle would say. She didn't know why, nor did she even question her odd expectation.

Her thought next flipped to little Elmo. Arlen had called to let her know that her number-one grandson was demanding chocolate-chocolate chip ice cream, a sure sign that he was on the mend. She hoped that he would like the singing get-well card she had sent. She offered another prayer of thanks for his improved health before her mind turned to her niece.

Carter seemed happier and more relaxed away from her own daily grind. Uncle Miltie was right: Willow's Bend fresh air, Gracie's own home-cooking and even the daily exercise she was getting, were obvious tonics. As was the blessed absence, over the last few days, of the dreaded motorbike.

Becky and Anna had already met again, Anna providing

welcome editorial and emotional support. Dennis McIver was thrilled to be supplying produce for Sunday's service and was calling Gracie each afternoon to update her on the daily status of the produce he'd be delivering.

Gooseberry yawned and reached out to bat her gently on the leg. She stooped, roughly stroking his orange tummy as he squirmed in delight. Then, in a flash, he wriggled from her grip, regained his feet and streaked around the fence into an alley. Straightening, Gracie chuckled, and calling his name, continued what was now a stroll.

Half a block away, she turned, shouted for him again, then waited. Seconds later, he meowed indignantly. Stretching, Gracie waited for another half minute until she heard rustling. Looking into the next garden, she spied Gooseberry attempting to push his way through a dense thicket of daisies. Laughing, she stepped toward him and reached down to assist. Scooping him under her arm, she ruffled his head, softly scolding him for trampling the perennial bed. As she plopped him onto the sidewalk, she noticed spots of black dotting his back and one white paw. Oil!

The Norton motorcycle!

Gracie dashed back down the street and into the alleyway. Half way down, partially-hidden behind the garbage cans, leaned a large yellow motorcycle.

He was here, within spying distance of her very own home! She spun and called for Gooseberry. An idea then settled into her mind during the couple of minutes it took her to sprint the block and a half to her driveway. It was simple— but she couldn't do it alone. Tumbling through the screen door, she startled her uncle in the midst of pouring his coffee.

"Hey!" he complained, "Where's the fire?"

"The bike!" she cried, pulling hard for breath. "It's in the alley, one street over."

He froze. "Did you see the driver?"

She shook her head. "Is Carter around?"

"Sorry, I think she's long gone."

"Thank heavens you're up. I need your help." She quickly told him her plan, rooting around in her kitchen drawers for the necessary implement. They headed to the old dark blue Cadillac, as quickly as Uncle Miltie could hustle beside her.

"It's not like you to damage private property, Gracie," he said, clutching his seat belt for dear life as they whipped out of the drive.

"My understanding is that it doesn't cause any damage, at least, it didn't for Arlen. Besides, I simply can't stand by and let this man stalk Carter."

"*Arlen* told you how to do this?" he asked, as she whirled the dark-blue car around the corner.

Concentrating, Gracie just replied, "I'm going to park here." She pulled beneath the shade of an enormous oak.

"The alley's got two entrances, you know."

She nodded. "We can't be in two places at once. I figure

since he parked closer to this end, he'll come this way. You stay in the car and keep an eye out. Yell if you see someone coming. Okay?"

"Got it."

Gracie glanced around and took a step.

"Wait a second!" her uncle snapped. "Do you *know* where to find the spark plug?"

Gracie rocked on her heels and shut her eyes.

"Thought not. The engine's underneath, near the front. Look for a cap, usually black, attached to a thick wire." Uncle Miltie held up his baby finger. "About this thick. Just tug the cap off to expose the plug. Careful, though! The bike's probably on a kick-stand. Don't lean on it."

She whispered her thanks and again looked up and down the street. The coast was clear. She slipped from the car, gently shut the door and hurried toward the alley.

Carefully edging around the trash cans to avoid making noise, she reached the motorcycle. Just as her uncle suspected, most of its bulk rested on a thick kickstand. Oil puddled in a perfect circle beneath, spoiled by a faint trail of paw prints.

Gracie slipped alongside, looking for the black cap and wire. There they were! She reached over, gripped the black cap with one hand and pulled.

Nothing!

She tried again, harder.

It popped off, revealing the spark plug's white porcelain insulator.

Her uncle bellowed. Immediately, a pair of voices floated down the alley.

Gracie ducked behind two cans. Closing her eyes, she breathed deeply. False alarm!

In a flash, she scampered back to the bike. After a quick check to make completely sure she was still alone, she dug into her pocket and dragged out the yellow lead pencil. *I know, dear Lord, I shouldn't be asking You to help me in something sneaky. But I wouldn't be asking if it weren't so important—so, please, let it be soft enough to work.*

She pressed as hard as she dared, biting her lower lip as she maneuvered the black tip over the insulator's uneven surface, drawing a line of lead up the entire insulator.

Yes!

Gracie quickly stroked several more overtop until satisfied with the uneven but continuous gray stripe. She grabbed the cap, ready to jam it into place when a thought struck her. What if returning it removed some of the lead?

For a moment, she froze.

Then, she positioned the cap gently, without shoving down, and stepped back. From a quick glance at the bike, nothing seemed out of place. She nodded, satisfied. Then, with a jaunty step, Gracie Parks, *saboteur extraordinaire*, strolled casually out of the alley and over to her car.

Eyes wide, Uncle Miltie leaned across to push open the door. "Took you long enough."

SO, HOW IN THE WORLD did you know that you can use a soft lead pencil to disable a motorbike?"

Gracie kept her eye on the street. "Because in his junior year of high school, my dear son and a couple of his friends dared each other to play a practical joke on their phys-ed teacher."

"Oh, oh. Over the years, teenage challenges like that have caused no end of trouble." Despite himself, Uncle Miltie started to smile. "The teacher probably wasn't too happy with our Arlen, I bet."

"Arlen felt so guilty, he couldn't eat or sleep for a couple of days. But he wouldn't say a word. I was worried sick, imagining he had some fatal illness. Elmo was much calmer, certain it had something to do with a girl. Of course, we were both wrong." She chuckled. "You know how, with teenagers, you never know when to push or let go?" Her uncle nodded.

"Well, hard as it was, we let it go. Then, after four miserable days, the poor kid cracked and told me all about it."

"What'd you do?"

Gracie drummed the steering wheel. "I called the principal and explained. We grounded Arlen for a month, and all three boys were all suspended for two days."

She slid down behind the steering wheel. "*Ssssh*, someone's coming!"

A tall man, dressed in dirty jeans and an old leather jacket, quickly approached from the opposite direction. He slowed down near the entrance to the alley, glancing around through his dark sunglasses, then disappeared down the alley.

Gracie bolted upright. "That's him!"

"Now what?" her uncle asked.

They heard the man grunt a couple of times, followed by what sounded like heavy springs rattling.

"It's working! He's trying hard to kick start it," Uncle Miltie surmised, "but can't get it going!"

Gracie turned Fannie Mae's key. They pulled directly across the alley entrance, then stopped.

Astride the bike, the now-helmeted man whirled. Seeing them, he spun back into position. With a vicious lunge, his boot slammed down on the starter bar. The bike shuddered, but the engine remained dead. Gracie whispered a prayer. He jammed hard again and again on his heel. The Norton Commando's kick start pedal flashed up and down to no avail.

"Yes!" cried Uncle Miltie as Gracie opened her door.

The man leapt off his bike. The Commando dropped onto the crushed stone with a tremendous *thump!*

"Wait!" Gracie shrieked. But he sprinted in the opposite direction, long legs barely touching the uneven ground.

She charged after him, despite knowing it was hopeless. Her heart sank as the distance between them stretched with every stride. The black helmet bobbed near the end of the alleyway when, suddenly, tires screeched and a small sedan shot across the alley, blocking the far exit!

Carter and Marge jumped out as the stranger pulled up short.

He turned. Gracie, now walking, continued deliberately toward him.

Carter dashed up to him. "Who are you? Why are you following me?"

"*Whhhat?* I'm not following you!" the stranger replied, his voice partially muffled by the half-raised shield. He turned and pointed at Gracie, who stopped dead in her tracks. "She's following *me!*"

Carter snapped, "Forget her. I'm an assistant district attorney, and I want to know your name."

"I don't care who you are! Get out of my way!" He took a step in her direction.

Gracie was suddenly at his shoulder. She had her hand on

his shoulder. "You've been stalking my niece. We want to know why. If you don't tell us, I'm calling the police."

He spun. "*Stalking her?* Are you crazy? I don't even know her." She stepped back, and it was then that Gracie noticed her best friend. Standing just behind Carter, Marge was staring at the motorcyclist's face, her mouth wide open.

The guy yanked off his helmet and shrugged. "Uh, hello, Marge."

Marge's mouth moved, but nothing came out.

"What's going on?" Uncle Miltie shouted, slowly making his way down the alley. "Who is he?"

Gracie shot Marge a look. "You know him?"

Marge nodded then croaked, "He's my brother . . . uh . . . my *former*, brother-in-law."

"Your *what?*" Gracie and Carter exclaimed simultaneously.

The small group stood quietly, eyeing each other, for a long moment.

"Might as well call it a day, son," Uncle Miltie declared to the man staring back at them. "You've been outwitted by Indiana's own Miss Marple."

24

"COME ON, BRETT," Marge urged the man sitting across from her on Gracie's living room couch. Much to Gooseberry's discontent, Uncle Miltie had commandeered the stuffed armchair near the window.

"We only want the truth," Gracie was saying.

"Just tell us what's going on," Marge finished.

Other than to ask about his daughters—who were on a sleep-over at the Cantrells's—Brett Reynolds had been silent during the short drive back to Gracie's, despite Carter and Gracie's efforts to get him to talk.

"What about the police?" he said finally, folding his arms across his chest. "You seem to think I'm some sort of criminal."

"Well, why did you run in the alley?" asked Gracie.

Brett's face reddened. "That was stupid, okay? I'm sorry. I looked up, saw you and panicked. I'd seen you before . . . with Marge and my daughters and, well, anyway, I didn't feel like explaining."

Marge glanced at Gracie and Carter. "Nobody's calling the police."

"Not yet," Carter added.

Brett looked stubbornly at them. "I've done nothing wrong." He locked eyes with his former sister-in-law.

"You almost ran over my niece!" Gracie cried.

"Whaat? Oh, that was *you*. Sorry, didn't recognize you," he replied. He spun to look at Carter. "You stepped right into the street. It wasn't my fault. Oh, come on! Marge, *please*, you know me. Promise not to call the police, and I'll tell the truth."

"You may look like you haven't changed, but the Brett Reynolds I *knew* wouldn't skulk around terrifying people."

He clenched his fists. "It isn't like that, you've got to believe me. Please, Marge?"

She was watching his face carefully. Her face softened. "Oh, all right," she said. "Everyone else agreed?"

"For the moment," Carter replied. "But if we suspect you're lying, the deal's off."

"You really *are* with the DA's office, aren't you?"

"Yes. In Chicago."

Brett placed his hands on his knees. "Just my luck. My

stupid bike quits on me for the millionth time and I get way-laid by some hot-shot lawyer, who, by the by, I am not, I repeat NOT, following."

"Well, you were following *someone*," Carter snapped. "You've been seen too many times."

"I said, I wasn't *following* anyone." He turned to Gracie, running thin fingers along his bristly chin. "Look, this might take a while. Any chance for a cup of coffee?"

She examined him closely. Brett Reynolds certainly didn't look like a typical stalker. But then, who did? Well, she had invited him into her home, and, after all, he wasn't a complete stranger. At least to Marge. So why would she be discourteous? Especially to her other guests. "Of course. Anyone else?"

Gracie's uncle rose with her. While she measured coffee, he filled the kettle. "What do you make of him?" he asked.

She hesitated before replying. Outside the open window, the grass glistened with the last remnants of dew. Two of the Griswold kids biked by on her quiet street, calling out to one another. Outside, everything seemed so ordinary, so *right*; but inside? Inside, Gracie really didn't know. One thing for certain, she hated feeling uneasy in her own home.

"I'm not sure. He appears genuine enough but . . ." Gracie stopped to pull out her herbal teas and dig around for a bag for Marge. Preferring orange pekoe, which she kept in an ironstone jar, Gracie prepared another pot as her uncle clumped to the table.

"His story makes sense," her uncle said, taking out oatmeal-raisin cookies. Gracie handed him a plate. "In a strange kind of way."

A few minutes later, the group was sipping from steaming mugs and sampling the cookies that Uncle Miltie carefully placed in the middle of the coffee table.

"Okay, Mr. Reynolds," Gracie said returning to her seat, "your turn."

"Thanks. Call me Brett." He took a long swallow. "Good coffee, thank you." He cleared his throat. "I'm not proud of it but . . . I've been watching my daughters."

"*Watching* Brooke and Emma?" Marge exclaimed. "Whatever for? Why didn't you just come to the house and see them?"

Brett hung his head and spoke softly. "You know why, Marge. I blew it as their father a long time ago. I've been fooling myself for years, trying to keep the girls out of my mind." He coughed self-consciously. "Couldn't really make it work, but I was afraid to come back. I figured the least I could do was not bother them." An uneasy smile slid over his face. "But, I figured, as long as their mother hadn't remarried . . ." he looked down, "there was a chance."

Studying his profile, Gracie sipped slowly and felt a tug on her heartstrings.

"I . . . I had some problems and . . . well, I'm the one to blame. I know that! I was a lousy husband and father," he said, his voice gaining volume as though he wanted to explain to the world at large. "I've got a good job now, and I've put my life back together. But then I heard that Adele was remarrying . . . and that the girls were going to have another father. Well, I guess I just freaked out. I wanted them to know *me* before they became some other man's children. I found out that they were coming to stay with you, Marge, so I jumped on my bike and came to Willow Bend."

"I still don't understand, Brett. Why didn't you just visit?" Marge asked.

"I . . . I almost made it to your front door. Then I saw them through the window." He lurched back and closed his eyes. "They are so beautiful! Almost grown up. They . . . they took my breath away." His voice filled with awe. "Emma . . . the spitting image of her mother, and Brooke." He laughed half-heartedly. "A bit like her old man but a thousand times better."

"Good heavens, man! Why didn't you knock?" Uncle Miltie asked. "You were right there."

"I know, I know, but I was terrified, overwhelmed really. I felt so proud, you know? I thought my heart would jump right out of my chest, but then I remembered how I'd left them. They were just kids and I . . . I, let's face it, I *abandoned* them. And their mother. They don't want to see me." Brett pounded the arm rest. "And, by the looks of things, they sure don't need me!"

"Don't be ridiculous. Of course, they do!" Marge replied. "You're their father."

He made a face. "Some father! My girls are better off without me." He turned to Gracie. "I can't blame them but, once I'd seen them, I just couldn't leave. At least, not right away. So, I watched them." He jumped up and began pacing. "I don't know. I've got this crazy notion that maybe if I got to know them a little, even from a distance, I might figure out a way to meet them."

He stopped and turned to Gracie's niece. "Look, Carter, I'm sorry if you thought I was following you. I never meant to scare anyone. Honest. I know I should've stopped outside Marge's shop. Made sure you were okay. But I panicked. I didn't want the girls to see me. I know it doesn't mean much, but I did stop around the next corner, and watched you get up."

"You're right," Gracie replied. "It doesn't."

Brett flushed even darker.

"So, you're *working* again?" Marge asked, refilling her cup. "Not in sales still, I hope."

The others exchanged glances at her tone.

Brett's expression froze momentarily. "As a matter of fact, I'm a wholesale buyer now."

"Oh?" Marge's business interests were peaked. "What do you buy?"

He ticked off a short list with his fingers. "Fruits, vegetables, specialty food items, you name it. I work for a chain that supplies upscale food markets and gourmet restaurants in the greater Chicago area. In fact, if it weren't for my darn bike breaking down, I'd have missed finding a hot new supplier right here in Willow Bend."

"Electrical problem?" Uncle Miltie asked.

Brett's face showed his surprise. "How'd you know?"

The elderly man chuckled. "Lucas electrics, right? In my day, we called them the Prince of—"

Brett grinned and joined in. "Darkness."

The two men laughed, breaking the remaining tension in the room.

"What's so funny?" Carter asked.

"The British built some wonderful cars and motorbikes," Uncle Miltie explained. "But they all had the same problem."

"They used Lucas electrical systems," Brett continued. "Notoriously unreliable! But I wasn't having any problems." He paused. "Until today, though."

Gracie felt a twinge of guilt. From the corner of her eye, she saw her uncle whistling quietly under his breath. They avoided eye contact. Gracie's mind was racing. First, she'd made a serious mistake. This poor man wasn't stalking Carter, and so she had had no right to tamper with his property. Adding to her predicament, she had never expected to feel sorry for the motorcyclist. Now, she would have to admit her culpability to a very nice man whose daughters she adored.

Fortunately, Brett didn't seem aware of her quandary. "Couple of weeks ago, the bike kicked the bucket outside town, near a farm owned by a nice young guy. Maybe you know him? Dennis McIver." They all nodded. "Great kid. Had the bike running in no time! Anyway, he let me help out in exchange for room and board. That way, I had an out-of-the-way place to stay and could easily zip into town to see the girls. And to top it off, Dennis is growing some amazing produce. I'm hooking him up with my company. He can't miss!"

He collapsed back into the sofa. "You know? I'm glad you ambushed me. I've been wanting to come clean but simply couldn't see how to do it." He downed the last of his coffee. "By the way, how did you know the electrics would go on my bike at that precise moment?"

25

THE LIVING ROOM was suddenly silent.

"We didn't," Gracie finally replied.

Brett leaned forward in his seat. "You mean, it was just a coincidence?"

"Well . . . not exactly."

"Wait a second, here." He leaned into Gracie's personal space. "Marge and Carter arrived later. If my bike had been working, I would have been long gone. Right?"

Gracie could practically feel his breath on her face, but she held her ground, returning his stare.

"So, you *had* to know the bike was immobilized." He turned to the others. "What am I missing? Mr. Morgan?"

Uncle Miltie shuffled uncomfortably in his chair.

"You're not missing anything, Brett," Gracie admitted. "I tampered with your spark plug." She stood quickly, moved to the hallway to her jacket, which hung on a hook. She reached down into a side pocket, pulled out the pencil and returned to her guests.

Brett frowned while Carter and Marge reached forward for a better look.

"It's just a pencil," Marge said. "I don't get it."

Brett took it from Marge's hands. "Well, I'll be! Where'd you learn this trick?" he asked, his eyes shining in reluctant admiration.

Gracie swallowed, surprised by his respectful reaction. "My son. It's an old story—but he once used it on a teacher's motorcycle in high school."

"I don't understand," Carter said. "How can a pencil disable a motorbike?"

Brett looked at Gracie. She shrugged. "I'm not too sure of the mechanics involved, but the lead line affects the spark. Only temporarily, though."

Brett nodded. "The spark's attracted to the lead. Instead of traveling down the middle of the plug to the engine, it whips along outside on the lead line. Without an inner spark, the engine won't start. Very simple to fix. You just have to wipe off the lead." He gave Gracie a bemused look. "Got to hand it to you, Mrs. Parks. It's a pretty neat trick."

"I'm sorry, Brett," Gracie replied. "It was wrong."

"Forget it! I'm glad you did it. You can't imagine the relief of being in the open." He hesitated for a moment before continuing. "Now, I feel a bit better about asking you and Marge for a favor."

Marge glanced at Gracie. For an instant, Gracie's stomach lurched at a startling new thought: if Brett wasn't following Carter, then who was?

"Maybe you two can help me figure out a way to make contact with the girls. I'll do anything in return. Just name it."

"*Umm.* I'm not sure," Gracie replied, dragging herself back into the conversation. "What do you think, Marge?"

Her best friend looked thoughtful. "Really, Brett. I don't see why you can't just come to the house, like everyone else."

Brett shook his head. "No, it would be too much of a shock for them. It wouldn't be fair. I'm only going to get one chance to make a good impression. I don't want to blow it. I was hoping to kind of ease into it. Something . . . oh, I don't know, some activity with more people around. To act as a buffer."

"I've got an idea," Gracie replied. She quickly told him about the Blessing Service and the need for minor construction help. "You give my church a hand, and we'll make sure you meet Brooke and Emma in the perfect family environment."

Brett surprised her by reaching over to give her a quick hug. "That's great! I can't thank you enough, Mrs. Parks."

"Hey, wait a second!" Marge replied, feigning insult.

"What about me? We were the back-up troops, ready and able and there in the nick of time."

Brett chuckled. "I've missed you, Marge." They both laughed, joined by the rest of the room.

"That reminds me," Uncle Miltie said. "What in the world were you two doing there, anyway?"

"I'd forgotten a change of socks," Carter replied. "I was just coming up the road when Marge rushed across the lawn."

Marge picked up the tale. "I happened to catch a glimpse of Gracie *sprinting* up the street."

"And the rest is history," laughed Carter.

"I'll be right back with more coffee," Gracie now told them.

"I'll give you a hand," Marge replied, moving to join her.

"What do you think of all this?" Marge whispered.

Gracie shrugged. "I was going to ask you the same thing. You know the twins better. How are they going to react?"

"I don't know. Not having seen them for a while, I've been afraid to mention their father. Do you think you could ask them?"

"Me!"

"Yes, you!" she said. "You've been a big hit with them and it would seem more natural for you to ask. Come on, Gracie," she pleaded. "You know I'd do anything not to hurt my nieces, but I'd hate for them to miss a chance to know their real father. He's basically a nice guy. You can see that for yourself. He doesn't deserve to be continually punished for his past." She took a breath. "Will you at least give it a try? For the girls, if not for me."

Two cups of coffee in her hands, Gracie hesitated in the doorway to study Brett Reynolds. Carter was explaining her marathon training and, though he was listening intently, his deep-set eyes darkened now and then, as a tiny shadow of defeat flickered across his features. Then something her uncle said made him laugh. His eyes suddenly glowed as a beautiful smile softened his face; for that brief instant, Brett Reynolds appeared on top of the world.

It was a remarkable and precious transformation.

"I'll do my best," she replied.

26

"S HE REALLY IS BEAUTIFUL, isn't she?" Brooke Reynolds said, pushing the glider gently.

Gracie stopped fussing with Gooseberry's collar and followed the teenager's gaze. She smiled.

On the opposite end of the porch, Carter leaned against the railing while chatting with Uncle Miltie. At her side, the gas barbecue glowed softly, and Gracie could see waves of heat rippling in the calm evening air. Partially-cooked hamburgers and hot dogs lined the grate, which sizzled and smoked every time Carter added Gracie's homemade barbecue sauce. Marge and Emma stood at a nearby table, laughing and tugging open a bag of fresh hamburger buns.

"She is," Gracie replied, inhaling the delicious aroma of outdoor cooking. Marge had been right. After Carter had taken Brett to Durant's Garage, Gracie's best friend had suggested that a casual cookout might be the perfect setting to question the girls about their father. Gracie turned back to Brooke, noticing for the first time that the teen had her blond hair cut in the soft, layered style preferred by her niece. "And so are you. That cut really suits you."

Brooke blushed and examined her nail-bitten fingers ruefully. "She's so confident, Mrs. Parks. She really seems to have it all together." She reached across to tickle Gooseberry's paw. The cat looked contented. "Why couldn't *I* be like her, the way Emma is?"

Gracie covertly prodded her cat until he squirmed and slipped into Brooke's waiting lap. "What do you mean, dear?"

Brooke rubbed Gooseberry's soft forehead. He purred and happily pushed against her. "Emma knows *exactly* what she wants. Always has." She leaned back and sighed. "I never do. There are so many possibilities, I just can't make up my mind. I bet Carter never was like this."

"Now, Brooke, you're being too hard on yourself. Nobody expects anyone to make final life decisions at fourteen."

"Maybe, but Emma's so much like mom, it's like they're talking a secret language sometimes. I don't seem to fit or even know where to start."

Gracie felt the girl reaching out for help, almost as if she'd extended her hand toward Gracie. "Do you ever think of your father?" she asked, keeping her voice deliberately light.

Brooke's eyes opened wide. "My dad?" she replied in a whisper. Then she nodded quickly. "Yeah. I do."

"And does Emma?"

The teen chewed what was left of her index fingernail. "Not much," she replied softly. She glanced at her twin to make sure she wasn't looking, then added, "Says he betrayed us."

"What do y—"

"Anybody hungry?" Uncle Miltie called, his voice shattering their intimacy. Gooseberry leapt up and streaked off the porch. Marge and Emma jostled good-naturedly while strolling to Uncle Miltie's side as Carter gently slid the cooked meat onto a platter. "Come on, you two!" he added, pointing a skewer in their direction. "We've got two cheeseburgers with your names on them."

"Coming!" Gracie replied, taking Brooke's hand. "We're starving, aren't we, Brooke?"

"So, *you're* the one with the Norton," Paul Meyer said early Friday afternoon, leading Gracie and Brett into his small office.

Brett shifted his feet and nodded.

The minister asked them to sit, then settled in an office chair behind his untidy desk. A bicycle helmet perched near the edge. "Boy, that brings back memories."

They looked at him.

He riffled fingers through his sandy hair. "Any trouble with the electrics?"

Both Gracie and Brett gulped before simultaneously bursting into laughter.

Paul's blue eyes blinked rapidly. "What's so funny?"

When she could catch her breath, Gracie replied, "It's a long story, Paul. Perhaps Brett will tell you sometime."

"I take it, Pastor Meyer, that you have some experience with British motorcycles?" Brett added dryly.

"Please, Brett, call me Paul. No, *my* English rose had four wheels." He leaned back in his chair, obviously remembering. "A British racing-green Spitfire I had in college. Loved her to bits, but, boy, I never knew when she was going to start!" He chuckled and pointed at his bicycle helmet. "These days, I get around under my own steam." He hesitated. "Any chance I—"

Brett grinned. "My old gal's right outside. We can go for a spin whenever you want." He glanced in Gracie's direction. "That is, unless Mrs. Parks has an objection."

Paul frowned. "Gracie? Why would you—"

Quickly, Gracie interrupted. "Brett's offered to help with the service. He's very handy and thinks he can build us a platform, isn't that right, Brett?"

Brett nodded. "I've already spoken to Dennis McIver. We've just pulled down an old plank fence. It'll be perfect. If you can give me an idea as to size, I'll head back to the farm and get started."

Paul rose and shook Brett's hand. "Why, that's wonderful. Just wonderful! I can't thank you enough. We were getting down to the wire." He shrugged sheepishly. "I was almost at the point of hammering something together myself."

Gracie's eyes widened. Paul had purchased a twenties-style stucco fixer-upper, halfway between Gracie's and the church. After several false starts at renovating, the unmarried pastor had to admit that, unlike his father, his hands were more skilled at preaching than building.

"Don't worry, Gracie," he added. "I hadn't even dug out any nails. Come on with me. I'll show you the layout."

Thick, puffy clouds blocked the sun as they strolled along the lawns and side parking lot of Eternal Hope Community Church.

"Why not use the front steps?" Brett asked as they strode onto the front lawn.

"The whole front side will be in full sun that time of the morning," Paul replied. "I'm afraid it'll be too hot."

"How about over here?" Brett suggested, moving off to one side.

He quickly took some measurements and made a couple of suggestions as to the width and depth of the platform and steps. As they walked to his bike, he tugged on his helmet.

"Guess we should postpone the ride," he said, checking his watch. "I'd like to get out to the farm, load, and bring the lumber back right away."

He and Paul shook hands. The bike started on the first kick. He leaned across and shouted to Gracie, "Thanks, Mrs. Parks! I think this'll be perfect." Brett flipped up a thumb and then roared out of the parking lot.

"He seems like a nice man," Paul said, as they watched his silhouette disappear. "Perhaps a little troubled. Where'd you find him?"

Gracie paused, not only impressed at her young pastor's innate ability to recognize someone in need, but at his confidence to express it. Three years ago, when he'd first arrived at Eternal Hope, Paul Meyer hadn't fully trusted his pastoral instincts. Indeed, on several occasions in the past, he had revealed his fears of inadequacy and self-doubt to Gracie. But, now, with the support of Gracie and others in his flock, he was maturing into a perceptive and confident spiritual advisor.

"Oh, Carter and I just ran into him in town," she replied, crossing her fingers at the small deception. "He's been helping Dennis out for a couple of weeks."

"Well, he sure is the answer to our prayer," Paul said, opening Gracie's car door. "It's awfully good of him to help out."

Gracie slipped in behind the wheel.

Paul leaned in. "Do you know what's troubling him? Is there anything I can do?"

Gracie smiled and started Fannie Mae. "That's kind of you, Paul, but you already have."

27

LATE SATURDAY AFTERNOON, Gracie stuffed several bags of groceries she had just picked up from the Willow Mart into Fannie Mae's back seat and climbed in the front. Overhead, the sun gleamed in the western sky like a huge pearl. She paused for a moment, collecting her thoughts. Preparations for the Blessing Service were nearing completion; inside her grocery bags were napkins, a variety of cheeses, and other last-minute ingredients.

Gracie had decided on using two simple salad dressings to top Dennis' greens. And construction outside the church was going well, with Brett planning to add the final coat of paint that evening. Later Marge and the twins would join her after dinner to make animal-shaped sugar cookies. She fingered the car keys. Everything seemed to—*Bang!* Something thumped the passenger door.

"Oh!" she cried involuntarily, startled at the noise.

A small grinning face, peered into the window. "Hi, Mrs. Parks!" Katie Nickolson shouted, her braces flashing in the sun.

Gracie smiled and leaned over to completely roll down the window. "Why, hello, Katie! You scared me."

"Apologize to Mrs. Parks, young lady," a woman's voice commanded. The girl obligingly said "Sorry!" then started to play with Fannie Mae's aerial. Phyllis Nickolson was pushing a stroller up to the window. Her freckled face dropped to Gracie's sightline. "Oh, dear, Gracie. I'm sorry. She didn't mean to frighten you."

"I know," Gracie replied cheerfully. "No harm done. How are you all?" She peered down. "My! Isn't Darren getting big!"

Phyllis smiled.

"I'm bringing my pony, Ruffles, on Sunday," the girl said, now skipping in circles.

Gracie raised her eyebrows. Phyllis gently shook her head.

"I didn't know you had a pony."

"Well, it's not a *real* pony," Kate explained, stopping suddenly to prod her baby brother. The baby giggled. "But my mom said Pastor Paul could bless my bike, didn't you, Mom?"

"I don't see why not," Gracie replied. "I've seen your bike. It's pretty special."

Phyllis tossed her a grateful look and grabbed her daughter's hand. "Let's go, now. Mrs. Parks is a busy woman. Thanks, Gracie. See you tomorrow."

Gracie chuckled the whole five minutes it took Fannie Mae to roll her home. *Well, dear Lord,* she silently mused while braking in her driveway, *I'm not entirely sure that blessing a child's bicycle is exactly what You had in mind for tomorrow, but You certainly can't doubt the sincerity of Your congregation's beliefs!*

"Oh oh. I'm not so sure about this one," Emma said later that evening, holding up an oddly-shaped sugar cookie. A freshly-baked batch rested on a hot plate in the middle of Gracie's kitchen table. Standing at the counter, Brooke giggled and returned to her pastry rolling.

"Oh, dear," Marge replied, wiping her hands on a dish towel. "The neck's too fat, that's the problem." She took a tentative bite. "It's yummy, though," she added.

"What's it supposed to be?" Uncle Miltie asked, peering over his newspaper.

"A giraffe," Emma replied, holding up a chunk. "Here."

He chewed. "*Mmm!* So what's the problem?"

"We can't serve broken cookies, Uncle Miltie!"

"Well, of course not." He rose and peered at the cookie sheet. "I guess that means we get to eat them, right?"

"Don't anybody panic," Gracie said. She picked up the

cookie cutters and eyed each critically. "As cute as these zoo animals are, Marge, I think we have to stick to the simplest, fattest shapes." She extracted three from the small pile. "Rabbit, hippo and fish. They're nice and round!"

Marge broke in, "By the way, where's Carter?"

"With Don." Gracie looked up at the clock. "I expect them any time, now."

Her uncle told the girls conspiratorially, "In that case, I'd better get my fill. Don could eat the whole lot."

They giggled.

"Enjoying yourself?" Gracie asked Emma.

Emma nodded and pushed a sheet of cookies into the oven. "I really like doing stuff in the kitchen. Especially when we can eat it!"

"Is your mother a good cook?" Uncle Miltie asked. He regarded the cookie he was about to bite into with critical appreciation.

Both girls nodded. "She's not big on desserts, though," Brooke replied. "Not like our—"

Emma frowned. Brooke looked unhappy.

"Why can't we talk about him?" Brooke asked her twin. "It's not like he's dead or anything."

"He's gone. He *left us*," Emma replied. "End of story."

Gracie held her breath for a couple of beats. The oven timer dinged. "Better check on those, Emma," she directed softly.

Emma deliberately looked away as she donned the oven

mitts. Brooke yanked a hunk of dough out of her bowl, slapped it onto the counter and began frantically rolling.

"Yoo hoo!" Carter's voice called from the doorway. "Something sure smells good."

No one replied. Marge glanced at Gracie. Uncle Miltie shrugged.

A moment later, Carter entered the kitchen. Pulling off her sweatshirt, she collapsed into a vacant chair. "Well, isn't this one big happy family!" she said, looking around.

28

A T THAT MOMENT, the phone rang.

Both Gracie and her uncle moved immediately, but Gracie was quicker. "Hello?"

"Gracie Parks?"

"Speaking."

"Hello, Gracie! Jim Riley here. How are you enjoying your niece's visit?"

Gracie nodded at Carter to let her know the call was for her before replying, "Very much, Jim. I just wish you could let her go more often." Carter excused herself and headed to the living room.

The lawyer laughed. "She's much too valuable, Gracie. I hope you don't mind my calling? I've got some good news. I tried her cell phone, but I guess she turned it off. Is she there?"

"She's just come in. Hang on," she replied, as Carter picked up the extension.

"Jim Riley?" Uncle Miltie asked.

She nodded. "Something about good news."

Uncle Miltie looked at the twins, who remained standing at the counter, still ignoring one another.

"Well, girls," Gracie said confidently, grabbing another rolling pin, "we've got several more dozen to bake, so let's get going, shall we?"

"Great news!" Carter yelled, practically dancing into the kitchen. She gave her aunt a kiss on the cheek, then, with a guilty glance, picked up a cookie from the platter. "They've caught him!"

"Who?" Brooke asked.

"Oh!" Carter hesitated. "Uh, sorry. It's nothing, not important."

"What's not important?" Uncle Miltie cried. "You haven't been this happy since you got here."

Squeezing his shoulders, Carter shot Gracie a warning look. "It's no big deal, honest. I'll tell you later."

Caught him, Gracie thought. She must mean her stalker. Emma and Brooke were staring at her. Gazing at their puzzled young faces, Gracie decided that there could be no harm in being open now. The world *was* a dangerous place.

"Carter, honey, I think you should tell us all now."

"But, Aunt Gracie, what about the girls?"

"That's exactly why," Gracie replied. "Why don't we all take a break?"

Brooke and Emma, still looking angrily at one another, sat down. Marge stood protectively, behind them.

"Well?" Uncle Miltie demanded.

"Why not start from the beginning?" suggested Gracie.

"Okay," Carter paused, collecting her thoughts. "You see, there's been some guy doing weird things for the past few weeks. But I didn't know who it was."

"You were being stalked?" Marge demanded.

"It started innocently enough with a bouquet of flowers delivered to my office. The accompanying note read, 'From a Secret Admirer.' I know that doesn't sound very threatening, and I must admit, at first I didn't think it was. I was a even little flattered."

"*Hmm,*" Marge said. "I wonder what I would have thought. Probably the same."

Uncle Miltie lifted his eyebrows. "She'd have tracked him down right away is what she means."

Carter ignored him and continued. "Then, more flowers arrived, followed by chocolates and stuffed animals, always with the same inscription. I asked everyone I knew if they were sending them, but no one admitted it. And then . . . then—"

"It got a little scary, didn't it?" Gracie offered, by way of explanation.

Spellbound, the others just held their breath.

Carter's expression was calm but her voice was tinged with emotion. "Yes. It got a little scary. He left a . . . disturbing message on my answering machine."

"You poor thing!" Marge exclaimed. "What did the police say?"

Carter shrugged. "Nothing they could do. You see, he hadn't really threatened me in any way. At least, not in a way recognized by the courts."

"But, he was . . . frightening you!" Marge blurted. "People just can't go around doing that!" She looked at the other adults. "Can they?"

"It seems that they can," Gracie replied. "I've spoken to Herb about it and he says the same thing."

Carter looked at them all gravely. "But it's over now. Jim just told me. Before I came, I gave him a tape of the phone message. He played it for the gang at work last week, but no one recognized it until one of our law clerks—who'd just returned from vacation—identified it!"

Gracie exclaimed, "Praise the Lord!"

Uncle Miltie clapped his hands. "Amen to that!"

"Who is it?" Marge demanded.

Carter's lips pursed. "It's so stupid! I should have recognized him on my own, but I was too distracted by how it made me feel. I couldn't look around me and see things clearly."

They all stared.

"It's someone I see almost every day—one of the security guards at the courthouse."

"Well, I'll be a monkey's uncle," Uncle Miltie said.

"And he's in custody?" Gracie asked.

"Well, he's admitted to sending everything. Says he never wanted to hurt me. His company's consented to move him to another building and to provide him with some professional help. He's promised to leave me alone if I agree not to file a harassment lawsuit against him."

"And?" Gracie looked troubled.

"The truth is, Aunt Gracie, I don't want to be a person taking someone to court. I'm a lawyer. I see troubled people every day. The court's not always the answer. It can sometimes make things worse. This man, he obviously needs counseling, not punishment." Carter was thoughtful. "You know I said that I saw him every day?" Gracie nodded. "I did, but I didn't even notice him. He was just some guy in a uniform. It may sound funny, but I can't help feeling sorry for him."

Inwardly, Gracie smiled to see her niece exhibit such compassion in light of the distress she had experienced. Not only was she good at her job, she was good for it, as well.

"But he was stalking you," Brooke said. "That's really creepy."

"I know, but it seems that he's got no friends, no family.

No one to turn to when he's feeling lonely." She smiled. "I'm very lucky." She looked directly at the girls. "Brooke and Emma, take it from one who's been there. Don't ever be too angry with your aunt or your mom, if you think they're being nosy or too involved in your lives. Cherish it and be grateful. It means you are loved. Trust me. There's nothing better."

Gracie's heart swelled with pride and tenderness. She hugged her niece. "Now I think it's time you turned those legal skills to better use. Defend those cookies against the claims of certain elderly gentlemen or we won't have any left for the Blessing Service!"

29

"OKAY, I THINK that's the last tin of cookies," Carter said. "Anything else?"

Uncle Miltie peered into the Cadillac's open trunk. "Good grief! You'd think we were also feeding the animals."

"Don't worry, dear," Gracie replied, glancing down her checklist, "just think leftovers." Gracie was confident everything was under control. She had risen early to finish her last two tasks: brushing Gooseberry and mixing the raspberry vinaigrette and the plain vinegar and oil dressing—both carefully chosen to compliment Dennis' salads.

"Yoo hoo, over there! We're packed!" Marge called, as she and the twins strolled across the lawn.

Uncle Miltie demanded, "What in heaven's name have you done to poor Charlotte?" he asked. Marge's little dog was yipping loudly, her compact silky body covered in brightly colored bows that jiggled with every movement.

Marge immediately grabbed the Shih Tzu and straightened the double ruby bow atop its spiky head. "She looks like a queen. Don't you, sweetie pie?"

Gracie grinned. "Everyone looks lovely. And you," she turned to her uncle in his crisp, white shirt and neatly pressed gray slacks, "you look very handsome." Everything had been checked and checked again—why was she uneasy? She thought for a moment. "Everything seems fine. We'll follow you, all right?"

Marge nodded and led the girls away. Carter slammed the trunk while Uncle Miltie maneuvered into the front seat. Shaking her head, Gracie returned to the porch to lock up.

"Meoww!"

"Gooseberry!" she exclaimed, reaching down.

Her cat stared up at her, his tail twitching angrily.

"Oh, my goodness! In all the excitement, I almost forgot you," she cried, scooping him under her arm. "Dear me." She stroked his head. "Imagine!"

A low rumble reverberated through the orange body. Fortunately, Willow Bend's finest feline didn't hold a grudge!

Although over an hour remained before the service for the blessing of the animals, the grounds of the Eternal Hope Community Church were abuzz with activity. The parking lot was already half-full. A number of children were shouting and yanking on leads, half-heartedly trying to control a quartet of howling dogs who were sniffing and pawing a pair of small crates. The two arch-backed cats inside wailed bitterly, which frightened a squawking bright green budgie caged nearby.

Over in a corner, a large truck was tucked partially in the shade under a stately oak, its broad rear doors emblazoned with a large bright red sign that read, "Caution, Live Animals" and a smaller bumper sticker commanding, "Honk if you're WOOLLY." Every now and then, the wooden sides would bang and shudder, followed by a barrage of lambs' bleating.

On the side lawn, Don, Lester, Abe Wasserman, and a couple of other men—their sleeves rolled up, their faces sweating in the humidity—were setting up rows of chairs. Slightly hidden under a pear tree, Brett Reynolds filled a number of buckets from a spilling hose.

Atop the freshly painted white stage, Paul paused to wave in the middle of directing people and their excited pets into chairs. Phil Murphy, the high-school band director, was on his hands and knees, fiddling with an electrical cable that snaked along the stage. Behind Phil's electric keyboard, positioned to the left of center stage, sat an obviously frustrated Barb Jennings. Phil motioned something with his arm. Barb's fingers flew over the keys, then stopped.

Lips tight, frown deepening, she vehemently shook her head in Phil's direction. The band director again jiggled the electrical connection.

As Gracie and crew began unloading, she stopped to watch Brett Reynolds, his face partially shielded by an old cowboy hat. He stood motionless. Then he twisted, tanned face glowing in the sun.

For a brief second, Gracie caught her breath. Poor man! Brett's raw expression had been a mixture of anxiety and longing as he watched Marge's van edge into a space and his twin daughters jump out. He pushed his hat lower and slipped further into the shade. Gracie and Marge had agreed to let him pick the moment to meet his daughters, so now Gracie said a quick prayer and turned her thoughts to removing cargo.

It didn't take long to carry everything into the church's kitchen, where Eleanor and Becky were waiting for them. After bringing Gooseberry—who was solemnly surveying the world from within his carrying crate—into the cool kitchen, Carter looked to see what other help her aunt might need.

"Can we take Charlotte and Gooseberry?" Brooke asked.

Marge paused in the middle of counting forks to smile at her nieces. Then, she raised a questioning brow in Gracie's direction.

"Sure," Gracie replied. "Hang onto him, though. He gets a bit spooked in crow—."

But the girls had already bolted for daylight, each clutching a squirming animal. With a quick salute, Uncle Miltie excused himself and clumped after them. As the door slammed shut, a mixture of sounds—yelping, yelling, and grunting—trickled into the kitchen.

"Hello, ladies!" a man's voice shouted. Dennis McIver leaned against the kitchen door, a large box in his hands. Both Carter and Becky moved to help him. He handed it to Carter. "I've got a couple more in the truck. Becky?"

By the time the young couple had returned, Gracie and Eleanor had already peeked inside the first box. It was stuffed with clear plastic bags each containing a mesclun mix, a medley of tender, young greens ready for washing and tossing, topped by brilliant crimson teardrop tomatoes.

"What do you think?" Dennis asked. He handed each woman a handful of fresh sprouts.

"*Umm*," Marge said, munching delicately.

For Gracie, the peppery taste was a dead giveaway. "Radish?"

Dennis grinned. He spun and dug again. "How about these?" he asked, handing over long white stems topped by bright greens.

Carter chewed slowly. "No idea, but they're delicious!"

The leaves looked vaguely familiar, but Gracie couldn't place them or the novel flavor.

"You'll never believe it," Becky laughed, holding Dennis's arm. "Sunflowers!"

For a few minutes, they happily poked into the overflowing boxes, delighting in the amazing variety of new produce Dennis was cultivating.

"Hey, Gracie, don't you have this in your garden?" Marge exclaimed, picking up several hairy leaves.

Gracie peered closely. Marge was right. She grew borage for its tiny, striking blue petals.

"There's a cornucopia of plants, especially herbs and flowers, you can eat," Dennis replied, closing the boxes. "It just takes a little imagination."

Eleanor embraced her grandson. "This is fantastic, honey. I'm so proud." She stood back, beaming. "Wait until your father and grandfather see this."

Dennis' face tightened. "Thanks, Gram, but I'm sure not holding my breath." He turned and gave Gracie's hand a vigorous pumping. "Can't thank you enough for this opportunity, Mrs. Parks." He glanced at Becky. "This means a lot to me."

"To us," his sweetheart shyly added.

Outside, about fifty noisy people and their excited pets were already squirming impatiently in the audience. Gracie immediately spotted Jessica Larson, clutching a fish bowl for her son Jeffrey, who was teasing a hound dog two seats over. Brooke and Emma were near the front, hanging tight to their adopted pets. Sitting nearby were Anna and Joe Searfoss. Gracie smiled and waved. Anna's face was alive with excitement as her husband held her hands and described the goings-on to her.

Near the stage, Frank Billingsly, his hands holding the reins for an old dappled Percheron, was chatting with Herb and Marybeth Bower, and Corey and Casey. Paul and Don were gesticulating wildly and shouting directions, in an attempt to assist an ancient farm truck into a double-wide slot.

Rocky casually strolled by, his dogs smartly turned out in their colorful neckerchiefs. And then there was Tuska, trotting happily on the end of a neon-pink lead. The piglet squealed, which caught Rover's interest, and soon Rocky and the Billingsly boy were laughing while struggling to untangle their respective beasts.

"Oh, my!" Gracie said, when she finally stopped laughing. "This is better than I'd ever hoped."

Marge could only stand next to her, staring around in silent awe.

Suddenly, something orange streaked out from the audience. Emma and Brooke leapt up, screaming. Gracie's heart lurched as her cat peeled down the middle aisle, nearly sideswiped by Rocky's lunging dogs. Gooseberry halted, spun miraculously, leapt up onto an astonished Linda Cantrell's lap, pounced over her shoulder and hit the grass running toward Frank Billingsly's horse. By now, the noise was practically ear-splitting, and several people were on their feet, chasing their own startled pets.

With an elegantly fluid motion, Gooseberry gathered his legs under him and magically sprung into the air, landing neatly on the old stallion's neck. Frank shouted. The Percheron whinnied and shied sideways, flipping Gooseberry ever higher. As Gracie blinked in amazement, her orange daredevil dropped safely in a nearby pear tree, all four white feet gripping bark.

Everyone, including the animals, roared in approval.

Sensing his audience's rapt attention, Gooseberry puffed himself up and deigned to glance down as if to say, "Want to see me do it again?"

"What are we going to do?" Uncle Miltie called, making his way through the chairs.

Estelle, already in her choir robe, called out, "Hey, you guys! You'd better hurry."

Gracie glanced at her watch. Ten to eleven! Paul was on the podium, his palms outstretched, encouraging his flock to take their seats. There wasn't much time. "I guess nothing for the moment," she replied, glancing at her now-calm feline. "He'll be safe for a while up there. But keep your eye on him, okay?"

Uncle Miltie gave her a thumbs up and settled into a chair directly under the pear tree. Gooseberry looked in the other direction.

The rest of the choir was pulling on robes, chatting excitedly. Barb tapped her baton against the door frame. They silently filed onto the stage. Once Barb was settled behind the keyboard, Pastor Paul strode to center stage.

Gracie took a deep breath and looked out over their motley audience. A sea of eager faces, both human and animal, stared back. Sitting with Carter, her uncle waved his cane, Rocky grinned from the fourth row, and she thought she glimpsed Gooseberry acknowledging her with a flick of his white-tipped tail. A rush of love and gratitude swelled her chest. *And God said: Let the earth bring forth the living creatures in its kind . . . let us make man in our image and likeness; and let him have dominion over the fishes of the sea, and the fowls of the air, and the beasts . . . And God saw that it was good.*

To her right, Barb's fingers moved and joyous music issued forth. Gracie smiled, then opened her mouth, preparing to sing.

THE SOPRANOS' VOICES floated into the blue sky, swiftly followed by the altos and tenors. *All creatures of our God and King, Lift up your voices, let us sing.* A single baying hound joined in just as the powerful baritones began a slow, steady round of alleluias, punctuated by a swelling piano rhythm. Paul waved to the crowd and soon everyone was singing along, including the lambs and several cats.

Trying hard not to grin, Barb kept control, both of her own expression and of her choir members, and her steely gaze held back the higher voices. Suddenly, the choir director's shoulders dipped, her right hand leapt forward, and Estelle's voice rose out above them all: *"Bright burning sun and golden beams, Pale silver moon that gently gleams."* Gracie took a deep breath, along with her fellow singers. *"Al-le-lu-ia, Al-le-lu-ia, Al-le-lu-ia, Al-le-lu-ia, Al-le-lu-ia!"*

By the time Barb played the final flourish leading into the last verse, a number of attendees were on their feet, clapping and swaying with the beat, eagerly awaiting their turn. The animals, growing used to the proceedings, paced or shifted restlessly and, apart from a sporadic wail or whimper, were surprisingly quiet.

The entire choir sang the last verse, their combined voices filling the churchyard and beyond. *"Let all things their Creator bless, And worship God in humbleness, Al-le-lu-ia, Al-le-lu-ia! Praise God the Father, praise the Son, And praise the Spirit, Three-in-One: Al-le-lu-ia, Al-le-lu-ia, Al-le-lu-ia, Al-le-lu-ia, Al-le-lu-ia!"*

"Alleluia and welcome!" Pastor Paul called out happily. "Wasn't that divine?"

The cheers were thunderous. Something near the back of the audience glimmered. Gracie grinned as she spied young Katie Nickolson slowly wheeling her bright red bike.

"We are gathered this splendid summer morning to praise God, the creator and giver of all, and to bless and give thanks for all His wonderful creatures, some of whom are here with us today." He looked around. "Seeing all your faces, I know there's not a single soul among us whose heart has not been touched, whose life has not been improved, by the presence of one of God's living beasts or birds. Or fish." He added hastily, noticing the Larsons. "This wonderfully reaffirms something that our dear friend Gracie Parks and I discussed.

You see, she was a little concerned," he turned and nodded to her.

"Admitting some doubts to me, doubts as to whether we should be celebrating the lives of animals when there are many human lives needing our support and prayers. In her heart, Gracie knew that this service was a good thing, but she wanted to be sure. I think you'll all agree with me that our heavenly Father would be proud of what we are doing today. I believe that He would applaud our efforts and be hopeful, knowing that His children care, not only for humankind, but for all His wonderful creations."

The young minister stepped down to walk among them. First, he shook Jeffrey Larson's hand and peered at his gold-fish. "And God said, let him have dominion over the fishes of the sea . . ." He paused, stepping between two chairs to reach a pony-tailed girl and her budgie. ". . . and the fowls of the air" . . . he added, as the bird cooed softly.

Paul's eyes darted across the crowd, a grin spreading across his face as he noticed Frank Billingsley and his son. In a couple of smooth strides, the pastor was kneeling beside Tuska. The piglet squirmed and grunted. ". . . and the beasts, and the whole earth, and every creeping creature that moveth upon the earth. For they are all God's children and today, we come together to ask our dear Father to bless each and every one of them."

As he strolled back to the temporary altar, he paused

frequently, ruffling a furry neck and chatting softly with the owners.

"Dear Lord," he began again, "we thank You for the gift of life, for the beauty and wonder of creation."

"Glory be!" a voice rang out.

Paul nodded and continued. "We thank You for the richness of animal life; for fish and birds, insects, reptiles and mammals." He glanced at Barb, who motioned to her choir.

Al-le-lu-ia, Al-le-lu-ia, Al-le—luuu-ia!

"We thank You, dear Father in heaven, for the animals here today, for each and every one has given us companionship, joy when we are happy and comfort when we are sad. Thank You for calling us to care for these creatures. As we honor these animals, may we learn love and respect for all living things."

"Amen!" voices sounded out.

"And now, if you would approach the altar, one by one, with your animal, we will begin the blessings. Those of you with larger beasts, don't worry. I'll come around to bless them." He nodded to Emma. Hesitating only slightly, she rose and, carrying Charlotte tightly, marched to the front.

Marge winked at Gracie.

Paul laid his hand on the little Shih Tzu and said, "O God, who has made all things, we pray You bless this dear animal, Charlotte; that she may be to all a source of joy and comfort and that we care and provide for her. Amen."

Charlotte yipped and wriggled excitedly, almost jumping

from Emma's grasp. Phil Murphy directed her to return to her seat, using the outside aisle.

One by one, the others took their turn, carrying or leading their beloved creatures forward, identifying it by name before Paul's waiting hands. The blessings flowed without a hitch until Jeffrey Larson's turn. Following the blessing, he was returning to his seat when he got accidentally bumped from behind. A stream of water sparkled in the air, followed by a flash of gold.

Patsy Clayton shrieked, rocking back in her wheelchair, as the tiny fish flopped into her lap, twitching and gasping. On her right, her father reached quickly across, gently scooping up the writhing goldfish. He rose and quickly slipped the startled creature back into its watery home.

"Is it my turn?" a young girl's voice cried. Katie Nickolson slowly walked her bike up the center aisle.

"Of course," Paul replied. "And, who's this?" he asked, touching the ruby finish.

Katie's braces glittered. "Ruffles. My pony."

Paul grinned and quickly blessed the noble steed. Then, he moved off to the side and blessed a trio of lambs, the Percheron and Ben McIver's calves and Eleanor's hens. Just as he was about to return to the altar, Uncle Miltie cleared his throat. Carter smiled.

"Yes?" Paul asked.

The elderly man pointed into the branches of the pear tree.

Paul looked up, only to find a pair of glittering green eyes blinking down at him. He chuckled. "It seems we have a reluctant participant. Come on, Gooseberry." He stretched out his hands. "Come on, boy!"

Gooseberry looked curious but wary.

"Okay. Have it your way," Paul said, then loudly repeated the blessing.

"Amen," Uncle Miltie shouted.

Suddenly, Gooseberry leapt from his perch and dropped with a *thump!* into Paul Meyer's open arms. The pastor laughed and carried him back to the audience. Brooke stood up and relieved him of his now-squirming parishioner.

"I thank you all for coming and sharing this precious day with us. I would also like to thank Eleanor McIver, Rebecca Baxter, Pat Allen, Bre—uh, and Carter Stephens for their help." Polite applause. "Following the last hymn, we will be serving light refreshments, including I understand, some fabulous fresh produce contributed by Dennis McIver. Thank you, Dennis." More clapping. Dennis' face turned as red as the tomatoes he'd brought. "And lastly, a special thank you to Gracie Parks for the idea for this wonderful—" he turned to Gracie. "—might I suggest *yearly* event?"

Loud cheers went up.

Blushing furiously, Gracie stepped forward and bowed.

Barb raised both arms. The congregation settled back down. As accompaniment, the old horse blew out its breath with an explosive snort. Hands still in the air, Barb grinned. For a moment, the air was silent, then Rick Harding advanced forward, his mellifluous tenor softly soaring into the sky. *"Each little flower that opens, each little bird that sings, He made their glowing colors, He made their tiny wings."*

Rick stepped back into place, winking at his young daughter, who was waving from her perch on her mother's lap.

Gracie and the others patiently waited for their entrance note while Barb's fingers raced over the piano. With a collective breath, they opened their mouths and sang the well-known refrain. *"All things bright and beautiful, all creatures great and small. All things wise and wonderful, the Lord God made them all."* A number of voices from the audience joined in, swelling the volume of the last line.

More voices joined in for the refrain. By the time Rick and Estelle had finished their alternating solos, the entire congregation was on its feet, in anticipation of the well-known verse.

Their uneven but united voices, fused with a variety of boisterous animal tongues, steadily swelled into wave after rippling wave of rising glory. Long after the choir and audience had stopped singing, the animals continued to vocalize, their barks, howls and whimpers urged on by the shimmering echoes.

And God saw all the things that He had made, and they were very good.

31

EVERYONE WAS ON THE MOVE, dragging, lugging or coaxing recalcitrant animals into the protection of their respective crates, cars and cages. Taking her gaze in a different direction, Gracie noticed her uncle. His attention was fully occupied by the sight of something happening farther down the parking lot. He was watching Rocky, whose two dogs, Gent and Rover, were always happy travelers, even in their owner's tiny car. Gent's head soon was poking out from the sun roof, alongside Rover's dangling ears. Gracie amusedly waved a good-bye at them.

"Where do you want him, Mrs. Parks?" Brooke came up to her, holding tightly to a now-exhausted Gooseberry.

"Oh, Brooke, dear," she answered. "Thank you. I think he'll be safest in his carrier." She motioned with her hand. "It's still in the kitchen. If you'd be good enough to just pop him back in? I'll be there in a minute."

"Come on, Emma!" she shouted to her sister who was

tugging on Charlotte's lead. The diminutive dog wouldn't budge. The day had obviously been too much for her.

"I'll help you!" Brooke, still clutching her own armful of fur, moved toward her twin.

Gracie watched the next scene unfold as though it were in slow motion. "Here," a deep voice said, "let me help." A man's hand suddenly reached down, grasping for the dog's collar.

Charlotte jumped, then flipped back her ribboned-head. Seeing the large figure looming over her, she gave out with a frightened yelp.

Face to face with the newcomer, Emma shrieked, "Daaad?"

Without warning, Charlotte bolted. Yapping ferociously, the feisty little Shih Tzu—all whirling ribbons and snarling teeth—launched herself at the interloper's ankles.

"Hey!" Brett Reynolds shouted.

"Dad? Daddy?!" This startled cry from Brooke, who had stopped in full flight, almost catapulting Gooseberry out of her arms. The cat wriggled and burst free, scrabbling across the uneven turf.

"Gooseberry, stop!" Gracie commanded. At the sound of Gracie's voice, her cat hesitated.

With a squeak, Charlotte scampered in the direction of her own mistress, who was now walking toward her. Marge scooped her up and cooed lovingly into a beribboned ear.

Emma's jaw finally worked. "Brett? Dad? Is it really you?"

Gracie looked for Gooseberry, catching a glimpse of his orange fur. He was continuing his retreat, leaping over a box containing a rambunctious Rottweiler puppy, and past a crate with three placid ducks.

"Daddy, Daddy, Daddy!" Brooke was screaming, running full tilt into her father's embrace. "I can't believe it's you."

"Brooke!" Brett dropped to his knees, his arms open. "Oh, my little Brookie," he murmured, running his hands through her hair. "Oh, my goodness, you're so beautiful!" He stood and stared. "Sooo *beautiful*. You don't know how much I've missed you."

Tears streamed down Emma's face as she struggled to maintain her composure. She stepped back, folding her arms then dropping them stiffly against her small chest. It was her duty, she felt, to challenge his sudden appearance and embrace from her twin sister. "She hasn't been 'Brookie' for years. Not that you would know, right?"

"Come on, Emma," her sister pleaded, twisting slightly in her father's grasp. "It's Daddy!" she added. Her tone was joyous. "He's back!"

Brett smiled tentatively. He extended his hand. "Emma," he whispered softly, clutching Brooke to his side. "Please, please don't hate me my sweet, sweet girl. Come here, my dearest. *Please!* I'm so sorry. You don't know how much I've missed you."

Emma's face crumpled, her body quivered. Tears welling

in her eyes, Gracie almost bit her tongue, straining to stop herself from crying out. The poor child was torn, part of her angry and holding back, part of her thrilled and longing to jump into his arms.

Brett said again, "Please, *please*, Emma. Just give me the chance to explain."

"Emma!" With a backward glance, as though afraid her father would disappear again, Brooke broke free, grabbed her twin and pulled.

Her face pale and disbelieving, Emma Reynolds collapsed into Brett's arms. For a long moment, they clung together in the sunshine, her dark head pressed into his chest. Then Brooke rejoined her father's embrace.

Watching their reunion, Gracie experienced a glorious shining moment spun from the golden threads of unceasing hope, absolute forgiveness and unconditional love. Never had she been more certain of witnessing the miraculous hand of God. *Thank You.*

32

"ISN'T THAT WONDERFUL?" Marge said, dabbing her eyes with a tissue. "I don't think I've seen Emma smile so much and Brooke . . . Brooke's positively *glowing.*"

Gracie looked out the window. The three Reynoldses were seated on the grass, lost in conversation.

"Gracie?" Paul's voice called, breaking the spell.

Gracie turned, searching the noisy crowd milling about outside the church kitchen. She found her young pastor, salad bowl in hand, seated at one of the long tables, along with the Searfosses, Rocky, Dennis and Rebecca. She waved happily.

"Delicious salad dressing!" Paul was shouting. His table-mates raised their forks and cheered. Rocky patted his shirt pocket, from which a sheaf of papers emerged, then gave her a thumbs up. Gracie's heart leapt. Wonderful! He approved of Becky's writing!

Marge smiled and blew her nose. She leaned closer. "Do you know what I felt when I saw them together, saw them rediscovering one another?" Gracie turned to face her best friend. "It felt like a real faith moment, you know? Like you read about in *Guideposts* magazine. Don't you think?"

Gracie nodded. She knew exactly.

"Wasn't that something?" Uncle Miltie was beside them, agreeing. "I wouldn't have missed seeing those girls meeting their father for the world."

He looked at Gracie and Marge. "I don't think Brett would have found the courage without both of you." He noticed suddenly that Gracie wasn't eating. "Hey? Aren't you even going to try a salad? Everyone's raving about them. Hang on a second while I get you one."

"Well, Gracie," Eleanor McIver said, crossing paths with Uncle Miltie. "Everyone's enjoying themselves. And don't you worry yourself one little bit about the drinks. I've just checked again, for the umpteenth time. Seems to be more than enough." Her husband, Ben, marched behind her, two overflowing plates in his hands.

He looked dark. "She insists we try this," the elderly farmer said, nodding at his wife. "Never been one for eating food I can't even pronounce. More of a meat and potatoes man, myself."

"Oh, for heaven's sake, Ben," Marge replied, after swallowing a tiny, flavor-rich tomato. "It's just a salad. Look around you! Your son's produce is the hit of the meal!"

Ben glared at Gracie. "I see *you're* not indulging."

"Only because I haven't had the chance, Ben, I assure you. I've already sampled Dennis's harvest and I love it! I don't think I've ever tasted such addictively delicious greens and vegetables!" She glanced at his untouched plate. "I was hoping you'd at least give them a chance."

Ben's mouth tightened. His wife sighed. Then, with a gasp of exasperation, she drove a fork into his colorful salad, loaded it and handed it to him.

Gracie continued. "I'll definitely start using those new, beautiful vegetables he's growing for my catering. People love to try something different."

The farmer's face reddened slightly as the two other women also stared. "Oh, for goodness sakes!" he snapped, eyeing the fork. "Never seen such a foolish commotion! It's just lettuce!"

The three ladies waited.

After a couple of seconds of chewing, his jaw slowed and the lines on his weathered face softened. He took another forkful. "Hey, this stuff's not so bad," he admitted. "What's it called again?"

"Oh, Ben!" his wife cried.

Marge shook her head. They all watched him. He kept on chewing.

Gracie beamed. "Now, if you'll excuse me for a moment, there are a few things I've got to attend to."

Marge joined her at the refrigerator. "Can you beat that? After all this heartache, one bite and Ben's a convert!" She looked up with an expression of gratitude. "All of this must be His doing! First, Brett and the twins. Now Dennis and Ben. You should go tell the boy."

Gracie glanced at the younger McIver. Beaming, Dennis was standing and chatting to a continuing stream of admirers. She smiled. "I think he already knows." She paused. "Where's Becky?"

"I thought she was with Dennis."

"So did I," Gracie replied, scanning the throng. Finally, she noticed her, alone, leaning against the far wall. The young woman was sadly staring across the room at her boyfriend. "Oh, dear. Marge, I'll be right back."

Gracie hurried over. "Becky, dear, you're crying!" She took her arm and handed her a tissue. "Come with me."

Once settled next door in the peace and privacy of Pat's office, Gracie asked, "Now tell me what's wrong? Dennis's produce is a big hit, and everyone loves the salads. Why, even his grandfather was clearing his plate."

Becky leaned forward. "Oh, Mrs. Parks, I know he's a success. I never had any doubts. Ever." She started to sob.

Gracie was confused. "But isn't this *good* news?"

The girl's face was anguished. "For him. Yes."

"For both of you, surely."

She slowly shook her head. "I used to think so, many times even pray so, but . . . now my father's convinced Dennis to back off. I'm so mad at him, at both of them, Mrs. Parks. But mostly at my father. I . . . I think I even hate him!"

"No! Becky—" Gracie interrupted.

"It seems my dad had the nerve to drive all the way out to Dennis' farm, just to tell him that he wasn't good enough for me." She swung her now fierce gaze in Gracie's direction. "Who's he to judge? Answer me that."

Gracie opened her mouth, and Becky continued.

"You can't, can you? And to top it off, Dennis didn't even tell me about it! Can you believe that? My own boyfriend, afraid to tell me the truth. Instead, he calls and cancels our date. Says he's too busy. I offered to come and help out. I don't care about going out on dates. We're long past that kids' stuff. I'd much rather be out working in the fields with him any day of the week. But he says, no. I push him, trying to make him forget my father but . . ."

She laughed, without humor. "Finally, he snaps at me, shouting that he doesn't want to be an unsuitable suitor. I know he was trying to be funny, but . . ." She paused.

"Can you believe it? I . . . I was so taken aback, I was speechless." The tears reappeared. "Oh, Mrs. Parks, why are men so stupid?"

"Now, now, Becky, you honestly don't think either your father or Dennis is stupid, do you? Of course not. You've asked me, so I'll tell you. It sounds as if they're both acting misguidedly, because of their love for you, that's all."

Becky blew her nose.

Gracie reached over to squeeze the young woman's shoulder. "You're very lucky, Rebecca Baxter, to have a young man who's so fond of you that he would sacrifice his own happiness for something he believes is better for you."

"But surely he can't believe that we're better off apart? That's just plain ridiculous! We love each other. We should be together."

"Like your father, Dennis only wants what's best for you. He knows you're talented, Becky. *Very* talented. That you could be a great success in the business world. And that this success is what your parents want for you."

Becky jumped to her feet. "What about what I want, Mrs. Parks? When do I get to make my own decisions? I *want* to marry Dennis. I *want* to raise a family with him. I *want* to write stories about our lives together. Is that so bad?"

She didn't give Gracie a chance to respond.

"I'm twenty-three, for heaven's sake! It's my life, isn't it? If I don't want to make a gazillion dollars and dedicate my every waking moment to working for some soulless corporation, why should I?"

She began to cry again.

Well, dear Lord, I've tried to follow Your lead all my life and I'm grateful for each and every one of Your blessings. I know Your hand has directed mine on countless occasions. It was through praying that I thought of Anna as Rebecca's mentor and I'm sure You were just as instrumental in my giving her story to Rocky. Are You guiding me right now? Is this Your path for her, and am I the one to open the gate? It seems likely and I sure hope I'm doing the right thing.

"You shouldn't," Gracie replied simply.

It was as though Gracie had said something miraculous, something astonishingly brilliant, instead of something so obvious. Becky's jaw dropped. A glow entered her eyes. "That's *exactly* what I think, Mrs. Parks. Maybe my writing won't sell, maybe Dennis's farm won't be a long-term success—but I want the freedom to find out." She smiled broadly and clapped her hands.

"And it's about time I said so, isn't it?" Her expression turned suddenly wary. "Oh, by the way, did I hear you right? You said earlier that Dennis's grandfather *liked* his salads?"

Gracie nodded, sending a silent thank-you heavenward.

"Well, I'll be. An answer to my prayers!" Leaning forward to crush Gracie with a powerful hug, she whispered, "You're amazing, you know that? Thank you for everything! Now, Mrs. Parks, you just watch me!"

AS THEY RETURNED from Pat's office, Gracie saw Brett Reynolds, his twins standing on either side of him. They were obviously enjoying themselves. Suddenly feeling guilty for having abandoned her tasks, Gracie spied Marge and Eleanor and heaved a sigh of relief. Her two friends were chatting, while keeping track of the coffee urn and juice pitchers. Tish and Tyne were at the large sink, beginning to wash up, while Don, Carter and Lester were bearing stacks of empty plates and mugs. Estelle approached her, extending a tray of sugar cookies. *What wonderful friends I have! Thank You, dear Lord, for this and all Your other blessings.*

"Where have you two been? We thought maybe you'd gotten lost and were about to send out a search party."

Becky grinned and took a couple of cookies. "Funny you should say that, Mrs. Livett. I once was lost, but now am found . . . ," she sang softly. Becky bit into a cookie. "I'll see you later."

As she turned and strode away, Gracie realized that she hadn't mentioned Rocky's approval to her.

She opened her mouth, but the girl now was too far away, smiling and talking while slowly making her way through a clutch of friends.

"What was that all about?"

Gracie reached for a cookie. "Have you seen Rocky?" she asked, ignoring Estelle's question.

"Uh huh. Over in the corner with the Baxters. I'm not sure what's wrong with Fred. He's as prickly as—"

But Gracie was already on the move. Halfway there, she was waylaid by Brett Reynolds. Brooke and Emma followed, their eyes never leaving him.

"Gracie!" he shouted. He was practically floating with happiness. "I almost don't know what to say." His eyes glistened. "You'll never know how much you've done for me, for us. I can't thank you enough. Ever. If you ever need anything, ANYTHING," he added, whispering fiercely, "I'm your man."

"No thanks are necessary, Brett. Your daughters are lovely, and it was an honor to help you reunite with them. Seeing the three of you together is something I wouldn't have missed for the world."

"I'm so glad we caught you," Brett said. "I didn't want to leave without you knowing how much I appreciate your help." He hugged the twins to him. "I'm taking each of the girls for a ride and then Marge is joining us for supper."

"Chinese!" The girls cried simultaneously. "Celestial City!"

"I'm delighted for all of you," Gracie replied. "Now, take good care of each other. And give my love to Mrs. Chu at the restaurant."

As she watched them leave, she caught sight of her uncle waving frantically. He was at a table directly beside the one chosen by the McIvers.

"Where've you been?" he whispered, tugging her down onto the seat beside him. "I've been looking all over for you."

"Comforting Becky. Why are you whispering? What's wrong?"

He put a finger to his lips. "All heck's about to break loose, if I'm any judge of human nature." She stared at him, puzzled. "Look," he hissed, gesturing.

She turned and barely contained a gasp. Immediately next to her, Ben and Jack McIver sat, bolt upright. Both men were staring straight ahead, watching Rebecca's parents marching toward them. Fred Baxter's mouth was already moving, though, with the surrounding noise, it was difficult to clearly hear what he was saying.

In another direction, Gracie noticed Dennis. The young farmer's eyes widened. He hurriedly finished a conversation and began to maneuver around a giggling quartet of girls who were tickling a pair of tiny kittens.

Lastly, she saw Rebecca. Her whole demeanor was in contrast to that of her boyfriend. Becky's young face was calm yet confidently set, as she strolled through the middle of the crowd toward her parents.

Everyone arrived at the table at exactly the same instant. For a moment, no one uttered a sound until, suddenly, a cacophony of voices filled the air.

Nothing was intelligible for several seconds. Finally, Ben McIver's deep bellow could be heard above the rest. "Quiet! Wait a minute."

The voices died as the group exchanged sheepish glances.

"That's better. Now, how about all of you take a seat, okay?"

So far so good.

Something moved beside her. Gracie shifted as Rocky, a grin filling his rugged face, settled in beside her. "This is going to be good." She started to ask him why he'd returned to the Activity Center, but, instead, she decided she needed to be certain about one thing.

"You liked her story?" Gracie demanded, keeping her voice low.

Rocky flipped up a thumb. "First rate," he whispered. "Just as you said."

Uncle Miltie shushed them.

"Tell you more later."

They twisted around to watch.

"Grandpa," Dennis began, his broad hand raised, "I know

what you're thinking, what you're going to say. But we've been through this a thousand times, right? I've got to be honest, I really—"

"Hold it!" Ben McIver commanded. "Son, I'll bet you your acreage that you haven't got the foggiest notion what I'm thinking."

Dennis blinked uncomprehendingly.

"Listen carefully, because I don't go back on myself too often." He glanced over at Eleanor who had moved in beside Rebecca. "Certainly not as often as your grandmother would like. Dennis, son, look, I . . . I was . . ."

He looked at his own son, Jack, who nodded encouragingly.

"Jack and I were just speaking to your hired help, Brett." Ben leaned forward. "Dark horse, that one. Seems he knows a whole lot more about farming than he let on, especially your kind. Told me about your deals in Chicago. About how fast your customer base is building and how much they like your stuff."

Ben leaned back.

Jack McIver took over. "What your grandfather's trying to say is that we were both wrong, son. And we're admitting it."

"From the moment I laid eyes on you," Ben added. "I guess I hoped you'd take over the family farm, just like your father before you."

Dennis opened his mouth.

"Now, hear me out. I've learned a whole lot today. Your

ideas on growing new products for different markets are right on the money."

He stood. Jack followed suit.

"From now on," Ben continued, "no more bickering. You grow what you think's right." He stuck out his hand. "Your dad and I, we're right behind you."

Blinking furiously, Dennis scrambled to his feet. He gravely shook hands with his father and then his grandfather.

"My turn," Rocky whispered, before rising. After gently touching Gracie's shoulder, he strode over to Fred Baxter's side of the table.

"Hello, folks," Rocky interjected smoothly, motioning for Ben to regain his seat. "Sorry to interrupt, but I think you'll be interested in what I have to say." He turned to Becky. "Especially you, young woman."

Becky looked startled.

"I've got some good news." He slid two sets of papers from his breast pocket and flattened them on the table. "This is a delightful descriptive memoir written by one R.J. Baxter." He smiled. "Known as Becky to those who love her. Gracie gave it to me to read. She said, and I quote, 'I think it's remarkable and deserves to be published', end quote. Well, Rebecca, Gracie's right. This is one of the finest pieces of writing I've had the pleasure to read in a very long time."

Becky stared at him.

Rocky chuckled at her reaction.

"Oh, Becky!" her mother gasped. "How wonderful." She turned to her husband. "Isn't that wonderful, Fred?"

"Of course, dear," he replied. "We've always known she could write. But where does that get you?"

Rocky pursed his lips. "Ah, Frederick, my friend, that's where you are wrong."

Fred's eyes narrowed.

"This is the sort of real writing that makes a young author's reputation once they start catching the eye of national magazine editors." Rocky squinted back at Fred Baxter. "Your daughter's a real writer, but she's not a real banker. And you've got to stop being so stubborn and admit it."

"I'd say it's time these two young folks were getting married." Ben McIver suddenly broke in before Fred Baxter could reply.

Stunned, Dennis slipped back into his chair. "Uh, not here, Grandpa. Not now."

Becky's eyes slid over to watch her father.

Fred Baxter's cheeks darkened. "Never!" he snapped. "It's all well and good that Rocky says Becky can make money writing and that you've come to approve of your grandson's farming, Ben. He's a fine boy, I'll give you that. But marrying my Becky." He shook his head. "That's one merger that's out of the question."

Ben scowled. "What're you talking about? You think our Dennis isn't good enough for her?"

"Now, Ben," Eleanor began, softly admonishing him.

Dennis interrupted. "Hang on, Grandpa, you don't know every—"

Fred cut them both off. "It's all settled. Becky's going to work in Chicago. Rocky's opinion is one I respect, but it doesn't change anything." He squared his shoulders. "Don't you see? No offense, Ben, but she can't marry a farmer. It'll limit her options."

"That's what I was trying to tell you, Grandpa," Dennis said. "Becky's got other plans. Big ones."

Ben dismissed them both with a sharp twist of his hand. "Any young woman would be lucky to have my grandson as her husband." He turned and watched her closely. "Am I right, Becky?" he asked her.

She stood up slowly.

"Becky, wait!" Dennis pleaded.

Rebecca Baxter spoke carefully. "Thanks, Mr. McIver. That's the first time anyone's ever asked me for *my* opinion." She turned her focus onto her father. "Dad, I'm sorry but it's my life. I love you and pray that you love me enough to see that and to understand what I'm going to say." She smiled. "You're absolutely right, Mr. McIver. *Any* girl would jump at the chance to make a life with Dennis—except for one *very* important thing."

A look of bewilderment was shared by her listeners. Looking defeated, Dennis hunched lower in his chair.

Rebecca's eyes flashed. She reached for her sweetheart's hand. "He's mine."

Dennis glanced up in happy astonishment. "You're . . . you're sure?" he asked.

Her look was enough to convince him.

Dennis didn't hesitate. In an instant, Becky was in his arms.

Uncle Miltie squeezed Gracie's hand. Rocky slipped away and returned to their table.

"Oh, Rocky, thank you," she whispered, giving him a quick kiss on the cheek. "That was a wonderful thing to do."

"No thanks, needed," Rocky replied. "Honest. Someday that girl's going to be a national literary treasure, and you heard it here first."

Uncle Miltie grinned. "If it were me, I'd demand a week's worth of her chicken and dumplings and double helpings of peach-a-berry cobbler with fresh whipped cream for helping Fred Baxter see the light the way you did."

"That sounds delicious but . . ." Rocky looked momentarily troubled.

Gracie frowned. "But? But what? Come on, tell me."

"Well, I wasn't going to ask, but I've got to admit it's really kept on bugging me." He laid his hands down on the table. "All right. You've got to promise to answer me one question, totally honestly."

Gracie and her uncle exchanged puzzled glances.

"I'll do the best I can."

Rocky nodded. "Okay, here goes. Just how many secret admirers have you got, Gracie Lynn Parks?"

Gracie's lower jaw dropped. "How many *what* . . . ?"

Uncle Miltie was determined to figure it out. "Hey, wait a second here. *Secret admirers.* Why are you asking that?"

Rocky made a hurt expression. "Well, when a guy sends a gal chocolates—the most expensive in town, I'll have you know—the least she can do is to thank him. Although, maybe I shouldn't be surprised, considering what you did with those poor flowers."

Gracie was incredulous. "You?" she demanded. "*You!* You sent the chocolates?" She realized he must have not put her name on the card, never realizing she and Uncle Miltie would assume such a gift was meant for Carter.

"Well, of course I did! Good grief, woman, I would have thought that was obvious—that is, until I saw that huge bouquet thrown into the garbage. Then, quite frankly, I didn't know what to think, so I decided to keep my big mouth shut." Rocky paused, bending toward Gracie. "So, somebody else sent you yellow roses. My question stands, however. How many *other* secret admirers are there?"

Uncle Miltie looked at his niece. As soon as their eyes met, the pair both let out an hysterical whoop and practically fell off their chairs, laughing.

"Hey! I don't get it. Come on, you two! What's so darned funny about that?"

Gracie's Gazpacho Garden Soup

- ✓ 2 small-to-medium cucumbers
- ✓ 1/2 red bell pepper
- ✓ 1/2 green bell pepper
- ✓ 1 medium onion
- ✓ One 14 1/2-ounce can diced tomatoes, with liquid
- ✓ One 6-ounce can tomato juice
- ✓ 2/3 cup chicken consommé
- ✓ 1/2 to 3/4 cup red wine vinegar
- ✓ Salt to taste (optional)
- ✓ Chopped pimento (optional)
- ✓ Sprig or two of parsley
- ✓ Lemons (optional)
- ✓ Croutons (optional)

Peel and seed cucumbers; cut in chunks. Seed and chop peppers. Chop onion into chunks. Pour tomatoes, tomato juice, broth and wine vinegar into blender or food processor, and add vegetables. Blend a few seconds until smooth—but do not puree. (A little texture adds to the taste!) Pour into a tureen or pitcher, cover it tightly and chill well in the refrigerator.

Gracie says, "Before serving this cold vegetable soup, I usually add a little extra chopped cucumber that I've reserved, and for a special touch, I drain well a couple of tablespoonfuls of chopped pimento with which to garnish the bowls, along with a dusting of finely chopped parsley. Lemon wedges served separately make a nice touch, while a dish of help-yourself croutons will please the heartier eaters."

About the Author

NICOLA FURLONG makes every effort to steal time away from cycling, playing ice hockey, growing perennials from seed and devouring chocolates (mostly devouring chocolates) to slip a snippet of mystery and suspense writing into each day.

Born in Edmonton, Alberta, the sixth of eight children, Nicola was raised in the Canadian provinces of Saskatchewan, Ontario and Prince Edward Island. She received a degree in fine arts and psychology from Carleton University in Ottawa, and then, following several older siblings, scrambled up the bureaucratic ladder with the Canadian government. After the publication of a number of essays, articles and short stories, her first mystery novel, *Teed Off!*, was published in 1996. Later that year, she left the civil service behind to concentrate on writing fiction and serving as a consultant to fisheries and environmental organizations. Her second novel, *A Hemorrhaging of Souls*, was published in 1998. She recently finished a suspense thriller entitled *Thy Will Be Done* and is currently researching a sequel.

Nicola lives in Sidney-by-the-Sea, a small town on southern Vancouver Island, British Columbia. You can visit Nicola's Web site at www.nicolafurlong.com.

A NOTE FROM THE EDITORS

This original Guideposts Book was created by the Book and Inspirational Media Division of the company that publishes *Guideposts*, a monthly magazine filled with true stories of hope and inspiration.

Guideposts is available by subscription. All you have to do is write to Guideposts, 39 Seminary Hill Road, Carmel, New York 10512. When you subscribe, each month you can count on receiving exciting new evidence of God's presence, His guidance and His limitless love for all of us.

Guideposts Books are available on the World Wide Web at www.guidepostsbooks.com. Follow our popular book of devotionals, *Daily Guideposts,* and read excerpts from some of our best-selling books. You can also send prayer requests to our Monday morning Prayer Fellowship and read stories from recent issues of our magazines, *Guideposts, Angels on Earth,* and *Guideposts for Teens.*